STITCHES

BRICKHOUSE

Phoenix Publishing House, LLC
Publishers since 2016

This novel is a work of fiction. Any references to real people, events, establishments, or locales are intended only to give the fiction a sense of reality or authenticity. Other names, characters, and incidents occurring in the work are either product of the author's imagination or are used fictitiously, as are those fictionalized events and incidents that involve real persons. Any

ISBN: 978-1-955235-03-7

Published by:
PHOENIX PUBLISHING HOUSE
P.O. BOX 154855
Lufkin, TX 75904

SYNOPSIS

Whoever said, "One bad apple spoils the bunch" had the Yarbrough's in mind.

Clifford and Darcy Yarbrough are the founders of Lakewood Hospital Center. The only black-owned medical metroplex in the city of Houston, TX.

Cliff is the only surgeon to specialize in kidney and heart repair allowing him to secure millions. Hospital's around the globe seek him out for some of the most arduous cases.

He is fighting tooth and nail to maintain his perfect family image but his children's shenanigans make that impossible.

He will do anything, and I do mean anything to keep his Hospital in the forefront.

Darcy's gentle spirit can only keep him at bay for so long.

Family secrets become deadly when these lies begin to cut deeper than any of them could imagine. Can this family heal once they start to bleed out?

* * *

PLEASE LEAVE A REVIEW WHEN YOU'RE DONE! I WOULD LOVE TO HEAR FROM YOU!

ACKNOWLEDGMENTS

Lord, I thank you for my gift of writing.

Brickhouse

Prologue

I was at the table studying when my dad walked in from his second job. We only had one bedroom so I slept on the fold away bed. I was maintaining all A's in school to ensure I got scholarships. My father Emmit was a hard-working man but he was barely putting food on the table.

I told him over and over that I could quit school and help out but he refused. My dad never finished school so his options were limited. He also refused to let my mother work outside of babysitting the neighbor's kids here and there.

I don't now if his hair was receding because of his age or stress.

He walked to the refrigerator to get a beer.

"You keeping them grades up Cliff?"

"Yes sir."

"A man is only as good as his legacy. You will never be worth anything if you don't do whatever it takes to have something. I was too nice so now I'm stuck at the bottom. You have to be willing to rob, cheat, steal or kill of necessary to not end up like me son. Never forget that."

I seared my father's words in my heart and on my mind. I promised myself I would never end up like him.

My wife won't ever have to work and my children will be taught the same mission in life. They will understand you have to secure wealth and make your imprint on this world at any cost.

Chapter 1

BRECHELLE

Three Years Earlier

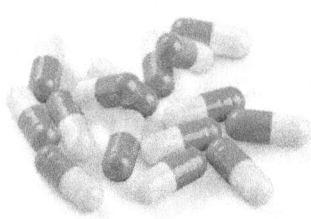

I traced the frame of my body with my hands. My ombre stiletto nails glistened against my black Gucci pant suit. I turned a lot of tricks to pay for this body and medical school. I wasn't born with a silver spoon in my mouth. At least an empty spoon would make me feel like I had a meal coming. I didn't like my mama rules, so I made my own.

The way I chose to take care of myself nearly left me dead on more occasions than I can count. I started tricking young so as I got older, I pretty much had a clientele. As I learned to keep up with my appearance and processed just how much sex sells my quality of John's got better.

I was able to stack once I got from under my pimp. Being in contact with that man was like having sewage explode on you and soak your white clothes to the bone.

Phillip Price was the epitome of greed and evil. He was the aftertaste of eating something on the verge of spoiling.

I ran my fingers through my fresh sew-in as if it would help pluck the traumatic memories from my brain, but they didn't. I still looked good though.

I was finally honoring myself by doing what I love most-practicing medicine and looking like a million bucks doing it.

My skills were so dope during my residency I had tons of letters of recommendation. I was still working at the hospital, but they couldn't afford to keep me. The ultimate goal was my own practice.

"You must be new?"

I tucked a lock of my raven colored hair behind my right ear gently brushing my diamond earrings.

They were a parting gift from one of my tricks.

Once I was done paying for medical school and my surgery, I got out the game for good. I wasn't putting my medical license at risk for anyone.

The man standing in front of me was slightly taller than me but what stood out most was his lips. They were already alluring but the way he licked them made them just sinful. My thoughts had me already repenting.

"Yeah, I'm new. How can you tell?"

"You have that spark in your eye that the threat of a lawsuit hasn't extinguished yet," he laughed. "I'm Kaimen by the way."

"Brechelle."

"Dr. Brechelle. I like it," he flirted.

"Excuse me," I told him stepping a few feet away to see who was blowing up my phone.

It was Parelle. When I was out on the streets it was me and Parelle. We both had dreams of getting out of the life, but some days Gemini would beat hope out of you. That was what they called Phillip on the streets. He would do his best to knock our teeth in if we ever called him by his government name.

Gemini didn't care if he pimped men or women. It was all about making a dollar to him. I knew I had to get away when the girls started getting younger and younger.

When I got my chance to get away from him that's just what I did. I'm going to kill Tamara for giving Parelle my number. We ain't all cool like that no more.

I pressed ignore and opened my Twitter app. I slid my fingers across my keypad until my message was complete. It was only seven words, but I was about to manifest them.

"You have me feeling like a stalker," I could feel Kaimen's sweet warm breath on the side of my neck.

"I was just letting Black Twitter know that you're my future husband," I stuffed my phone back in my purse.

"Is that so?" He flashed me those pearly whites bouncing on his tiptoe.

"It is."

"Okay so future wife let's blow this joint and get some real food!"

"Yes, let's."

We took separate cars to a quaint bistro near downtown Houston. I parked my old school Mercedes next to his big body one.

I was working my butt off to slide these buns into something just like it. I got this old one because it's what I could afford right now if I wanted to ride in something foreign.

Kaimen hurried out of his car to open my door.

"You have to lift up on it as you pull it," I yelled through the window.

My face felt feverish with embarrassment but Kaimen wasn't tripping. Once he finally got the door open, I stepped out. He grabbed me by the hand and escorted me to a cozy spot on the patio.

He waived to the waitress as we passed which let me know he was a regular here.

I know he better not be bringing me somewhere he brings all his potential chicks because I'm nothing like the rest.

"So, what is your specialty?"

"Gender reconstructive surgery."

"Shut the front door! Let me lock you down before you blow up," he grabbed both sides of his head as if he couldn't believe what I just said.

"I have some offers but no one is willing to pay me what I'm worth. I'm in the process of getting published."

"Already?"

"Yep."

"That's dope! I'm just a lowly Gynecologist," he joked. "My brother is a big-time plastic surgeon."

"Oh, that's amazing! I wonder if he can point me in the right direction."

"Write down on a piece of paper what you want to make."

"Are you serious right now?" I stopped eating my salad to discern if he was playing with my emotions. "You don't even know me like that?"

"You not sounding like a future wife right now," he slid the napkin over to me.

I pulled a pen from my purse and wrote the six-figure number I knew I deserved starting out.

"You foul! You see me calling you this entire time! You could've been dead or anything. You don't even care! Yeah trick I know where you came from! Straight out the hood!"

A tingling of adrenaline started course through my body. I know this Negro didn't come down here and clown me in front of my future baby daddy. You always find Parelle in the hood talking loudly, walking fast and lying to hustle upon a dollar.

There's no way I'm going to associate myself with him anymore now that I'm on my way to living the life I've always deserved.

Parelle was openly gay but he wasn't the clean-cut kind. After Gemini cut him loose, he just started doing strange things for a little bit of change.

Gemini ran his business like DCFS. Once you aged out of the system, he didn't want anything to do with you.

I slowly started to pull away from Parelle as I progressed in medical school. For some reason he feels I owe him something.

"Do we have to do this now?" I spat.

"Evidently we do! Hey mista' sophisticated man," he snapped his mouth open and flicked his tongue mimicking Ms. Pearly, the landlord on *Friday After Next.*

"NO...WE...DON'T!" I gripped his arm like a python.

"Get yo' hands off me lil'-"

"Parelle...please," my eyes pleaded with him to stop his verbal assault and display of ghetto theatrics.

He reluctantly followed me far enough away so Kaimen couldn't hear us.

"Look, I haven't been ignoring you. The dude I'm with trying to plug me with a job at the hospital. You know I need this P."

"Look, I know you in doing your doctor thing but don't forget who was in the trenches and knows the REAL you," he stressed eyeing me from head to toe. "And stop wearing that fake designer. It looks cheap. Let me get forty-dollars," he held out his hand.

I reached in my pocket and slapped the money in his palm.

"Now can I get back to this hustle?" I tilted me head to one side toward Kaimen.

I could see him out of the corner of my eye watching intently.

"Get our money boo," he clapped his hands and walked off.

I had no idea how he even got downtown but one thing I do know about Parelle is that he gone make something shake.

I need to disappear on him ASAP! I'm changing my number as soon as I leave here and taking down all my social media accounts. If I want a fresh start, I need to get low.

It was like cement was sitting in my stomach as I sauntered back over to Kaimen.

"Kaimen I need to-"

"You don't have to explain."

"No, I need to tell you something about me. About my past. I want you to know everything about me upfront. I don't want any secrets between me and my future husband."

"I've seen all I need to see. Sometimes when you outgrow people, they don't like it. As a matter of fact, they will try to pull you back in the barrel where they feel you belong. You handled that with poise and grace. Reminds me so much of my mother in tight situations."

"Thank you."

I wanted to let my skeletons out of the closet before I fell in love with this man but he wasn't trying to hear it. If he only knew...

Chapter 2

ALLACIA

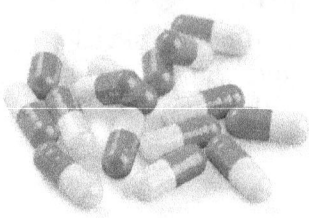

I rolled my eyes as Martine vented about her boyfriend's latest indiscretions. I've been telling her for years to stop dating black men. Dating white was the best thing to ever happen to me.

"Girl, I can't believe after Vonte dropped off that Henny lovin' last night. Man, we were going at it like savages for hours."

"You talking about that Henny lovin' lasting long. Have you ever tried pressed juice what grass shot pipe? It definitely hits different girl!"

"You know Vonte only drink Hennessey. Piss be smelling like ammonia."

"Yet you still screw him."

"I'm breaking up with him for real this time. I need to find some inner healing and get my vibrations up."

"All you need to do is leave that no good man you're trying to raise alone and you'll be alright," I badgered her. "I told you Niles has a friend that wants to meet you. Stop dumbin' yourself down and make these men come up and get it!"

"Girl, I'm all about black love and that's it. I don't have anything against those of you that have found it in other ethnicities but he would have one time to call me a nigger and I'm going to jail. Period Pooh."

"Girl, every white person ain't racist. Niles and I have had disagreements but he's never called me out of my name. You know why? Because he respects me even when he's angry."

"I guess," her response was dry and my cue to end the call. "I need to get waxed but my esthetician is always booked."

"I told you to use Nair. It's just as effective."

"Nair got chemicals in it," she snapped.

"Nair got chemicals in it but you screwing that nigga and going down on him and his mad dirty out here in these streets. On top of that you eat meat all them other processed foods so shut up! You weirdo!"

"Well, I need to get dressed so I can go surprise my man. He's been working late a lot so I need to drop off some good loving to him. I'll talk to you later."

"Okay. Talk to you later."

When the prominent Houston surgeon Niles Winchester asked for my hand in marriage, I almost took one of his eyes out trying to get that five-carat pink diamond on my finger.

He hands me over his black card without thinking twice. Once we're married in July, he's adding me on as an authorized user.

I was in medical school myself when I met him. I'm not the school type though. I'm the shopping type.

My father was livid when I quit but he'll get over it. The person that said that one apple spoils the bunch had my family in mind. Now depending on who you asked the bad apple will vary.

Personally, I feel my daddy Cliff is a bacterium filled piece of slime. He will do anything to protect his legacy. He chokes the life out of us with his demands. It's always all about the Yarbrough legacy.

I have a business degree already that allows me to do some consulting for small businesses. I help them get all their paperwork in order, guide them on how to set up their company, branding, and a ton of other stuff.

It was lucrative but not high profile surgeon lucrative.

My brother Ario always pushed for me to pursue my singing career but that's a high industry to break into.

Ario says that one if his patient's husband is a big-time producer and she promised me a meeting with him.

Singing just wasn't my thing though. I didn't love it like that. I wanted a man to take care of me like my father has done with my mother.

I haven't needed his money since Niles started taking care of me and I was relieved. My dad complained about every dollar he handed over to me even though I deserved it.

His money was really hush money if you want to keep it all the way real.

That man has so many skeletons in his closet it would make your stomach turn if they were exposed.

I pushed my boobs up in my dressed so that my nipples were barely inside. Niles liked when I put the girls on display. He would motorboat them every chance I afforded him.

I smiled as thoughts of my baby danced in my head. Niles favored Paul Walker. After the actor's death people stopped us all the time to comment on the strikingly similar resemblance.

It was after hours but Niles was on call at the hospital tonight. I rarely popped up but I've missing him like crazy since he's been working long hours at his practice and the hospital.

I decided to head to the on-call room just in case he was taking a nap. He wasn't in the E.R. when I got in so that where I was hoping he was.

I could hear moans on the other side of the door. I was sure it wasn't Niles until I heard his voice.

"I know you're not!" I burst through the door.

They didn't even have the decency to lock it! I was mortified by what my eyes were processing.

Niles was balls deep in some Becky with blonde hair. Her ice-cold blue eyes were bucked in shock as I stood in the doorway.

"Allacia," he panted pulling the sheet around him as he jumped from the hospital bed.

"Allacia what? What do you have to say? Better yet what can you say?"

"I can explain."

"Explain screwing some chick at work? Please enlighten me."

He stood there searching for a lie.

"I'm sorry babe."

"Sorry? You sorry alright!"

I started to pull my ring off but I earned every carat.

I slammed the door behind me and headed home to pack my things. I had enough money to get my own place but tonight it would be The Four Seasons.

I don't believe in second chances. Catching Niles in that compromising position ripped my heart out but I will survive this. I hope.

I never could imagine this happening to me in a million years. Here I was thinking because he was white, he had to be right. I guess dogs came in all breeds.

Chapter 3

CLIFF

Present Day

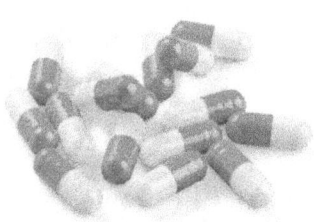

"Mr. Yarbrough, Mr. Winston is here to see you," Esmerelda one of my staff members notified me.

"Please escort him in."

"Mr. Yarbrough I'm glad we could meet on such short notice," Kenneth extended his hand.

KSSHHH! Was the only sound being heard when the vase fell.

Kenneth strong armed me pressing my face against my mahogany wood desk. I could feel the cold pistol tip pressed firmly against the back of my head causing a shiver to run down my spine.

I was hesitant about inviting him to my home but it was the only place I was sure he wouldn't try to kill me. I didn't want people at the hospital in my business so he couldn't come there!

I was relieved I followed my first mind. It was usually right.

"What the hell is your problem?" I grumbled careful not to yell.

The last thing I needed was Darcy barging in and seeing me hemmed up against a desk.

"You know what my problem is! The money my associates have charged you to clean has been coming up short! We overlooked the few thousands here and there but now we have over a million dollars missing! We've killed people for less!"

"Look it takes money to make money! I had to open more cash businesses to clean all the money you keep laying in my lap! It's not easy! I already have the IRS sniffing around and if I go down so do y'all!"

"Is that a threat?"

"No, it's a fact! Now get your hands off me!" I snatched from his hold straightening my clothes.

I rounded my desk and took a seat as I caught my breath.

"Kenneth give me a few months and I will triple what's come up short with interest."

"If we find out you used our money for that new expansion at your fancy hospital, they will be fishing you out of the Gulf of Mexico and that's a fact!"

"Baby...Oh, I'm sorry. I didn't know you had company," my wife Darcy was right on time.

I was out of excuses for Kenneth.

"It's okay honey. We're just wrapping up. I was just walking Mr. Winston out."

His face was set like stone and I know he wasn't happy I had ended our meeting abruptly.

"Mrs. Yarbrough, it was a pleasure meeting you. Cliff I'll be in touch," he cut his eyes at me as he walked out of the door.

The freshly mowed grass tickled my nose as I slammed the door behind him.

"My love what have you gotten yourself into now?" Darcy's eyes were filled with concern.

Her black long hair was pulled back to reveal a fresh, soft face. Those fiery chestnut eyes were set elegantly in their sockets, they have watched yearningly over our family for so long. Her smooth creamy Nutella colored skin graciously compliments her eyes. She was the epitome of what aging with grace looks like.

My bald scalp prickled with shame. I didn't know she heard what was transpiring on the other side of the door.

"Nothing that I can't handle baby."

"This hospital is not worth your life! Why can't you just trust what you've built?"

"Because what I've built cost money if we want to remain the top hospital in the Houston area. It's costing one point five million per bed to build in the annex. The five-hundred thirty-two beds in the original building cost eight hundred million total. That's not including the other buildings in the metroplex. We receive grants for being a teaching hospital but it barely covers a portion of our cutting-edge technology and equipment we use. I'm just trying to build something that will outlast me."

"But at what cost Clifford?"

"Dinner is ready," Esmerelda interrupted my response.

"Thank you. Have the kids arrived yet?"

"Yes ma'am. They are seated and waiting."

"Thank you," she told Esmerelda. "Cliff please try to be more supportive of them. Every week is seeming you are badgering them for something or other. I want these dinners so that we stay in touch with one another with our busy schedules."

"Yes dear. I will try. I need to make a quick call and I will be right there."

Support is not what these kids need. They need me strong arming them so they don't lose sight of my vision.

I often tell Darcy what she needs to hear. It has kept the peace in our marriage for over thirty-five years.

I pulled out my phone and scrolled until I found Tish's number. She has been the perfect escape for me the past year.

The love I have for her is different than the love I have with my wife.

I burn with passion for this woman. I crave her and there's nothing I wouldn't do for her.

She doesn't make things difficult and she stays in her lane.

Not once has she ever given me an ultimatum. That's what makes me spoil her.

"Hello," Tish cooed on the other end.

"Hey baby girl."

"Hey daddy. How was your day?"

"It was okay. I just wanted to hear your voice before I sit down for dinner. Be ready tomorrow because I'm taking you shopping."

"Awwee, thanks! I can't wait to thank you properly," she enticed me.

Her words were wrapping themselves around my heart and groin.

Darcy poked her head in the door again signaling for me to come on.

"Okay, well I will touch base with you later," I ended the call.

Tish knew when I ended calls that way that someone was around that I couldn't speak freely in front of.

My wife placed her hand in mine as I emerged from my office.

We made our way down the hallway to the dinner table.

"Glad you all could make it," Darcy greeted our children.

"Anything for you mama," Kaimen said.

He was our most well-rounded child. He was the blueprint for all my blood, sweat and tears over the years. Kaimen was the one who really got the just of what I was building. If he continued on this path, he would definitely be my successor.

"You are always sucking up. I guess you have to since you punked out and became a gynecologist. We all know you fold under pressure so it makes sense," Ario teased.

"Yet you still manage to run around with my sloppy seconds," he shot back.

I knew the young lady at the dinner table looked familiar. Ario knows these dinners are for family but leave it up to him to ignore the rules.

"Sloppy?" The young lady scoffed.

Brechelle was clearly irritated by the petty exchange of Kaimen's ex-girlfriend.

Ario was the best and worst parts of me. He was more arrogant than I ever remember being but he was justified. He's one of the most sought-after plastic surgeons in the country. He's made millions by doing what others say couldn't be done. I made him insure his hands for over a million dollars each and their worth every penny.

"Leave him be," I demanded Ario who returned my request with an eye roll. "Where is Allacia? She has no reason to be late being that she has no job!" I asked my kids who had bothered to respect me and their mother's time.

"I think she had some kind of an appointment," Ario attempted to lie to cover for her. Those two are thick as thieves.

No sooner than I had completed my sentence she came waltzing in the room.

"Hey y'all," she dryly said taking her seat.

"Don't come in here late and have the nerve to have an attitude lil' girl!" I snapped.

Her icy gaze stumbled upon me. I could tell she was biting the inside of her cheek.

"Ain't nobody got no attitude daddy! I just had a bad day!"

"The way you talk you would swear I didn't shovel out thousands of dollars on your education. Including the medical school, I pulled strings to get you in just for you to drop out and live off me and your mother!"

"Here you go! Then you wonder why I don't come around that often," she rolled her eyes.

"Watch how you talk to my daddy," Kaimen chimed in. His wife Brechelle touched his hand signaling for him to stay out of it but he ignored her.

"You know better than to say anything to me you slithering snake!" She spat at Kaimen.

"Mama and daddy think you so perfect but I know who you really are!"

I could see Allacia's body lock up with rage as she gripped the dinner knife.

"Snake? Girl, you're as useless as they come! Running around here living off mama and daddy money because you too lazy to work. Matter of fact you don't do anything but lay on your back! You need to beg Niles to take you back. Oh, that's right he went off and married that white chick from work."

"Watch your mouth before I run in yours," Ario stood to challenge Kaimen.
"You wouldn't dare risk damaging those mediocre hands," he laughed.

"Mediocre? Ask your wife how mediocre I am!" Ario took a step forward in Kaimen's direction.

"Don't put me in y'all mess! Ario how dare you imply anything other than us working together!" Brechelle defended her honor.

Those two were always lurking in a dark corner somewhere but that wasn't my business.

"Stop it! All of you just stop it!" Darcy intervened as she always did when we're together. "We're family! I don't care who shot John but y'all need to fix this! Your father and I won't be around forever and all you will have is each other! Stop this foolishness! Excuse me," my wife folded her napkin on the table and walked away.

"Look at what you've done! You upset your mother," I stood to go after her.

"Daddy," Allacia caught me halfway down the hall.

"What Alli?"

"My credit cards didn't work today," she whined.

"Yes, because I cut you off! You need to get a job! I'm not going to keep enabling you to squander your life away!"

"We both know why you're enabling me daddy! Should I march down this hallway and tell mama why?" She threatened.

WAP!

My hand came down across her left cheek as rage swept over me. I've never laid a hand on her before today but she's taking things too far.

"Don't you ever threaten me! You being cut off from my money will be the least of your worries! Now get out of my face!"

I left Allacia standing there holding her face in utter shock. I could see her body crumpling in on itself.

When I made it to the bedroom my wife was sitting at her vanity with her hand against her breastbone in tears.

"Baby, those kids always argue," I consoled her. "You know you can't afford to get worked up."

"I just wanted today to be the day we told them about my heart," the tears flowed from her eyes making me feel inadequate.

I was the only surgeon who specialized in heart and kidney issues but couldn't figure out a way to save my wife.

"I told you I will figure out a way to save you! You just must hang in there. I've created cutting edge procedures that have changed the face of medicine. I know I can save you!"

"Maybe God doesn't want you to save me."

"In that operating room I am god Darcy!"

"Watch your mouth. Pride goes before destruction and a haughty spirit before a fall. That's scripture."

I rolled my eyes at her.

"Are you coming back down for dinner?"

"I'm not hungry. I'm tired. I just want to lay down for a bit."

I kissed her forehead and helped her to bed.

We have been keeping her illness from the children. They are aware of her previous surgeries to repair her heart valve but they don't know their mother is dying.

Because of the conflict of interest, I couldn't operate on her. I'm sure if I had she wouldn't be suffering from advanced heart failure now.

After the repair, the muscles around the valve became too weak preventing the valve from closing tightly.

The only course of action I could convince her to take was getting on the donor list.

She's refusing any high-risk procedures to save her life. She doesn't want to risk having more time taken from her.

She's decided to just spend as much time as she has with me and the kids. It's the reason she started the weekly dinners together.

They think it's just their mom being mom but they don't know that her days are growing shorter and shorter.

Chapter 3

DARCY

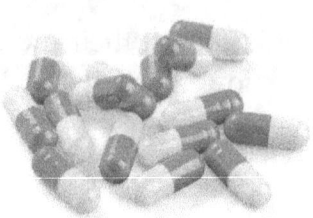

I was in turmoil on the inside. I clasped my hands together to stop them from shaking. I could feel time slipping away from me. My family was in shambles.

I know Cliff was on the phone with that Tisha woman. I've known about her for a while now.

I've been so sick I haven't been able to fulfill my wifely duties.

I was hoping she will be able to provide him some comfort after I'm gone.

Now back in the day I would've taken him for everything that wasn't nailed to the floor or bust his head open to the white meat.

Cliff knows I don't play. I remember back in college I found him sitting in the car with Bertha Reynolds.

I was a fool back in the day. I was classy but I didn't play at all.

I pulled up on them and hopped out the car.

"So, this is what you're doing?" I asked Cliff.

He was so shocked his mouth was just hanging open. I'm not sure if it was because I jumped out on him or because I had my forty-four pointed in his face.

"We weren't doing nothing Darcy," she interjected which pulled my venomous glare her way.

"Who asked you?" I snapped rounding the truck.

I pulled her door open and snatched the bottle of liquor sitting between her thighs.

KSSHH!

"Stay out of my business and out of this truck!"

"Get her off me Cliff!"

I was doing my best to rip her apart.

Now if she had kept her mouth closed, I wouldn't have put my hands on her. She was going to have to find another ride but my quarrel was with my man not her.

I chuckled as I thought about how crazy I use to act back in the day.

Death had a way of putting things in perspective.

Cliff is accustomed to being in control of everything. He can't control my heart failure so it's tormenting him.

Both of my boys are clawing to sit on their dad's throne.

Ario has so much bitterness inside and that's my fault. Cliff was always so hard on him because he acted just like him but I started to intervene.

The beatings were getting to be to brutal and he wasn't going to keep punishing my baby that way.

I feel like I failed Ario. We made a lot of mistakes as parents when we were young.

Kaimen is a perfectionist but he doesn't have what it takes to run a hospital. I love him and he's the fixer of the family but he's not strong enough to wield the power it takes to run that hospital.

My baby Allacia is just lost. I've been trying for years to get her to open up to me about what's pushing her over the edge.

After her breakup with Niles she just spiraled more out of control. Her hope of love got buried when that relationship ended.

I'm afraid I'll die without ever knowing the root of her pain.

Chapter 4

BRECHELLE

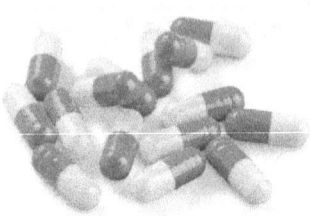

"Baby these dinners with your family are getting wilder and wilder. Yesterday was crazy! I can't believe he showed up with your ex. That was just tacky. Then he tried to throw me in the middle of that mess!"

"Don't worry about it baby. What's understood need not be explained. Ario is toxic. Always has been always will be. He hides behind his credentials but it's apparent he's still that insecure boy I grew up with."

"Enough of that. How about you give me something to make me a little lighter on my feet before I go into the office?" I slid my tongue across his neck stopping to nibble on his earlobe.

"Babe, you know I have to meet with my dad before I go in. I can't be late or he won't put me on his calendar the rest of the month."

"Geez Kaimen! I have needs too! I swear that man controls y'all every move!"

"Watch it," he warned me.

"I'm just saying babe," I whined.

It wasn't like he had far to go. We all live on what his dad calls the '*Yarbrough Estates*' except for Allacia, the rebel.

We have huge houses spaced out over the hundred and fifty acres of land. It's giving cult vibes for sure if he were to add mandatory bible study around this hell hole.

"After work I will do whatever you want. I promise," he kissed me while stopping to pay extra attention to my bottom lip. "Bre."

"Yes," I panted hoping he would negate his meeting with his father to take me up on my offer.

"You have until the end of the week to find an infertility specialist. I'm ready to start a family with you. I've been patient enough. Make it happen or I will," he said getting up from the bed.

I watched his perfectly sculpted body pass in front of me as he headed to the bathroom to shower. Kaimen was a tall cup of chocolate milk that I loved to indulge in. His fade was just as perfectly manicured as his nails. He manscaped but not enough so that it's creepy to look at when you're down there.

When I met him at a medical convention three years ago, I knew he was the one. What I didn't know is how hands on his father was. It's his way or the highway around here.

I'm just playing my part until I can get my husband from under him so we can start our own practice. He just needs to understand that it's okay to have your own dreams and build your own legacy.

Right now, I had to figure out how to give him a baby.

I ran my finger though my messy but perfect hair. My hydrated Brazilian bundles were accented with blonde highlights. I pulled the sheets from my body as I decided to get my day started.

I stood in the full body mirror admiring my physique. I was flawless. My size twenty-six waist gave way to a thirty-six-inch hips. I had all my work done before Kaimen but if I needed anything touched up, I know I could count on Ario to get me right.

Kaimen has been pressing me for months about having a child. I know I can't have kids but I never told Kaimen. I was scared he wouldn't marry me or love me the same if he knew my truth.

I decided to go through the infertility treatment but on my own terms. I had to control the narrative. It was the only way my marriage would survive.

"I'll check in with you for lunch," Kaimen said kissing me as he left to meet his dad before work.

"Okay babe."

I walked to the closet and pulled out a black plunge line Dolce and Gabbana dress and paired it with my choca leather black Christian Louboutin stilletos.

Something simple but sexy. I dealt with a clientele that would notice such things.

The six figures I wrote on that napkin when I first met Kaimen paled in comparison to the seven figures I was bringing in now.

I specialize in reconstructive surgery with a concentration in gender reassignment. I only came onboard at Lakewood Hospital Center because it allowed for an even larger bag to be checked. Let's just keep it all the way funky... I loved seeing the commas in my bank account.

Gender reassignment has always been a passion of mine but it didn't hurt that it was a very lucrative field.

I gave myself a look over in the mirror and headed out to complete my own task for the day. I pulled out my phone to call my bestie Tamara.

Breaking free from Parelle was like scrubbing funk from your body that's not yours.

I've had some work done to my face so I look nothing like I did years ago. I could walk past him and he wouldn't even know it was me.

Me and Tamara stayed connected because we have a different type of bond. It's rare and I cherish it.

"Tamara, I need you to meet me at the address I'm about to text you."

"Girl, how you didn't know I had something to do today?"

"Because you never have anything to do. Get your butt up and meet me. I need your opinion on something."

"Alright. I'll meet you there."

I jumped in my Mercedes-Benz A class and merged onto Interstate 45. I popped me a Xanax just so I could deal with these fools in morning traffic. By the time I get done with my errands I will be on top of my game to operate today.

I cut down a couple of side streets before I had to commit a homicide on this freeway. When I pulled up Tamara was already waiting for me.

"Girl why you got me sitting outside this empty building like a crackhead? Some old white lady came out here asking if I was you."

"Girl, shut up and get out of the car."

"What are we doing at this fancy office building?"

"Would you stop asking questions? Dang!"

"Mrs. Yarbrough?"

"Yes, thank you so much for meeting with me," I extended my hand to the realtor's.

"That's the white lady I was telling you about," Tamara's attempt to whisper failed terribly.

The realtor cut her eyes but didn't say anything. I was so embarrassed. Tamara was the only friend I had from my past. I knew I could trust her with my life and I always ran things by her. Ghetto and all.

"This will be your office. As you can see you have six patient rooms and a reception desk. The building and office are already wired and connected with cable and Wi-Fi. If you need a vendor for medical and computer equipment, I can give you a card to put in an order. Here are the documents if you would like to take them to have your attorney view them, you're more than welcome to do that."

"That won't be necessary. Where should I sign?"

"Here, here and here," she pointed to the pages that were flagged with red arrows.

My heart dropped at the thought of what I was about to do but I was willing to do whatever it took not to lose Kaimen.

"Thank you, Mrs. Yarbrough. Here are your keys. If you have any questions or concern you have my number. Call me for anything. I mean it."

"Thank you and I will."

Once she was out of sight, I turned to Tamara to bear my soul.

"Okay, spill it slut," she said. "You know you not about to leave your people practice, so what's up with this new building?

"Well, Kaimen has been pressuring me to have a baby."

"Well, we both know that's not possible, so what's the tea sis?"

"I'm going to set-up a fake fertility clinic. I helped a friend a while back in college who has reluctantly agreed to help me pull this off."

"You've always been crazy and known to make a way out of no way but this is going too far Bre! Now you are playing with someone's emotions. That can get you killed!"

"Look, I'll just pretend to go through the treatments. I have access to patient records; all I have to do is put my name on someone that's infertile complete with labs and voila!" I forced a crooked smile but Tamara didn't return the gesture.

"I wouldn't be a real friend if I didn't tell you that you're messing up. This is too much! Kaimen is an OB/GYN! Did you think of that? Matter of fact, he handles high-risk cases! How you gone explain some doctor coming out of the wood works to treat you?"

"You let me worry about that. Look I have to get to the office," I pulled Tamara into an embrace and locked up my new office. I had a few weeks max to turn this office into a full-blown practice.

As soon as I got into my car, I looked down to see an unknown number lighting up my screen.

This wasn't uncommon. Some of my clients had two or three phones and depending on what they needed, they utilized them all.

"This is Dr. Yarbrough," I spoke into my phone.

"Ohhh, you sound so professional," the voice on the other end caused my stomach to immediately turn.

I forced the vomit that came rushing up my esophagus causing it to tighten back down.

"How...how...did you get this number?"

"Don't worry about all of that. A better question is do your husband know about your past? Does he know how you really paid your way through school? Who you really are?"

I disconnected the call. My hands were trembling so bad I couldn't start my car. Tears stung my eyelids as my stomach bound itself in knots.

I closed my hands to form a tight fist and commenced to striking myself in the face repeatedly.

It was just something that I did from time to time when I was triggered.

How did Gemini find me?

I looked down at my phone again and the same number popped up.

"Hell....hello."

"Hang up on me again and I'm going to send these pictures to everyone in your family!"

The notification on my phone prompted me to check my messages.

I was mortified. Pictures of a person who no longer existed was plastered across my screen. I was so lost back then just finding my way. I was willing to do whatever it took to get through medical school.

I barely had a place to lay my head but I never missed a day of school. I was determined to get out of the hood and live the life I was built for.

Here comes Gemini trying to pull me back.

"You have two weeks to get me one-hundred thousand dollars," he demanded.

"I can't get that much money together in that amount of time! Are you crazy?"

"Well, you in that rich family of doctors living on that nice estate. I'm sure you can think of something," his laughed caused me to cringe.

"Okay, I'll get you the money but this is it! I want you out of my life!"

"It ain't it until I say so! Don't forget who you talking to!"

Gemini's rage echoed through the phone reminding me of the many beat downs I suffered at his hands.

I never came up short or left a trick unhappy but he still found an excuse to beat me.

I think he hated me most because I had to courage to live a life, he was afraid to.

I had to figure out a way to get rid of him. The more I tried to escape my past the more it kept popping up to gut punch me.

I was already stressed about this baby thing with Kaimen not this just adds more fuel to the fire.

I took the small glass tube with the black top from my purse.

I sprinkled the white powder on the cusp of my hand and inhaled.

When I exhaled, I could feel my body numbing all my problems.

I know it was only a temporary fix but I had to do what I needed to push forward.

So, cocaine it was.

I slid my tongue across my hand and tossed my head back on the headrest.

I was petrified of Gemini. Not just for what he could do to me but how he could expose me and ruin everything I worked so hard to achieve.

I couldn't believe this is happening.

Chapter 5

PARELLE

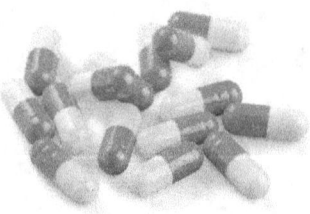

My jaw was locked so tight I could feel the pain from clenching my teeth. These heifers still clicked up after all this time but just gone cut me all the way out the picture.

Brechelle thought she was going to just get rid of me. She shut her social media down for a while but I knew where to find her.

She only goes to one nail shop in the city and there's no way she was going to switch up.

She was anal before she started making all that money. I know who the real Bre was and I was going to enjoy reminding her.

I pulled out my phone and redialed the last number in the call history.

The number wasn't saved but I knew exactly who it was.

"Hey, she is coming out. Go ahead and call her now," I advised him.

"Aight. Bet," he said ending the call.

Gemini wasn't too happy when I told him that Bre making some real money now and acting brand new.

He feels like since he never gave her permission to leave him that he's entitled to a percentage of what she's making now.

I've been following her and her family for nearly a year now.

I studied them all as much as I could to help Gemini implant himself in their lives.

Her sister-in-law, Allacia was easier to gain access to but I don't think sis have a job.

I had to start getting up early just to wait for her to start her day.

I know she's going to be our best way in.

I can't see a gynecologist and I ain't got enough money to book an appointment for plastic surgery.

I called and them thieves talking about a consultation appointment is two-hundred fifty dollars.

I wish I would give my coin up that easily.

I was comfortable in my own skin anyway.

"Yeah, beat yourself unconscious tramp," I said as if she could hear me.

Adrenaline started to rush through my body absorbing Bre pounding her face.

"Yeah, pick it up. You know better," I continued to badger Bre from my car.

I watched her hold the phone to her ear like a statue.

My girl was shooketh! Yeeasss!

My time to watch her squirm was up. The tracker I stuck under Allacia's car was showing her at the Wax Bar.

I'll go in there and get one ball waxed just to get close to her. My entire plan was hinged on baby girl not liking Bre either.

She looks like she stuck up to so I know they be clashing. I just need to stir the pot to cause an explosion.

I would set the ball in motion for Allacia to do all my dirty work.

I can just sit back with my popcorn and view the show.

"Welcome to the Wax Bar can I help you with something?"

This receptionist was giving me all kinds of attitude honey and I wasn't in the mood.

"Listen, you are paid to do a job! I will sit both these balls in your face with that crooked side part ponytail. Don't make me read you for filth because I will!"

"What's going on here?"

Another woman appeared. I guess she heard me gathering her employee.

"Your subordinate is up here acting like it's a violation for me to be in here. I'm trying to get my balls silky just like everyone else," I snapped my neck.

"I apologize. I can take care of you myself. You can have a seat and I'll get the room set-up."

"Thaaannnkkk you," I toggled my head from side to side like a bobble head.

My mama always told me to keep a slide across town. I guess Allacia's daddy got the same advice because he sure got one across town.

The girl that came out to help me reminded me of her.

You would be surprised by what a person really does when they don't know their being watched.

I was lurking on her Facebook to see if that was her while I figured out a way to strike up a conversation with Allacia.

She was trying to act like she was unbothered but she clearly was.

"I apologize for all that. I just hate when a person tries you for no reason."

"It's not my business."

"Are those shoes from the summer Chanel catalog?"

"You recognize them?"

A flash of excitement flashed in her eye letting me know I found my opening.

I couldn't afford anything in the catalogs I was obsessed with but my day was coming. Bre could've invested in me some bundles to sale or something. Left me in the gutter turning tricks while she rode off in the sunset to her new life.

"Girl I'm a gay man, what you think?"

We smacked each other's hand then erupted in laughter.

"I'm glad you checked her," she tossed her eyes towards the girl at the front desk.

I'm not sure who castrated her bang all the way back like that but it made her look more ridiculous.

"Please, I've had my share of people trying to discriminate against me. I gather them and be ready for the next. They not about to play up in my face."

"I know that's right."

"You look familiar. I think I've seen you in a picture with my ex friend Brechelle."

"Yeah, I know her. Ex friend, huh?"

"Yes, ex girl. She straight out of Garden City Apartments and started acting all funny once she started coming up. Mind you we've been friends for yeeaarrsss," I stressed.

"Whaattt?"

Allacia was all the way turned towards me now. Totally opposite of what her body language was saying when I walked in.

I could see my words swirling in Allacia's head as I poured her all the piping hot tea.

Every time she blinked her eyes it was as if she was taking another sip.

"Parelle," the lady who consoled me called my name.

"Look, I'm about to go. It was nice meeting you."

"Here, take my card," Allacia insisted.

I wasn't sure what this child was handing me a card to because I don't think the poor thing work.

"Oh, you're a consultant?" I asked her.

"Yes."

"Gone head. What type?"

"A little of this and a little of that."

She was a little of a lie.

"Okay. Okay. I'm going to call you. Don't start acting funny like you're lil' Sista in law," I waved the card around in a figure eight.

"I promise I won't! We gotta finish this boo," she smacked her lips.

Fish love calling the gay boys boo. Just extra. Like it's going to make us cooler or something.

"You know it."

The lady waiting for me shot me a noxious look trying to intimidate me.

"You know what? Y'all do too much in this lil ghetto spa. I'm taking my money to the Chinese people. At least they smile and talk about you in a different language."

The lady waved me off. She turned around without dignifying what I said with a response.

I was too thirsty to use the card I was just given but I had to play it cool.

It was like when you get a new number and you trying to figure out when's a good time to call so you don't look parched.

I figured I could wait at least twenty-four hours.

This girl fell right into the trap. Now it's time to start feeding her information.

Chapter 6

ALLACIA

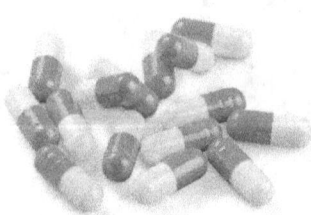

I purposely scheduled my therapy sessions the day after these God forsaken family dinners. I'm always triggered in some shape, form, or fashion.

I only attended out of respect for my mother. My dad recently cut me off hence the attitude I give him.

Ever since I dropped out of medical school, he's been impossible. I just woke up one day and realized that I'm working towards his dream and not mine. He didn't care when Niles was taking care of me but that was old news now.

I stalked his Facebook sometimes. He ended up marrying that tramp I caught him with while I ended up running back home to daddy.

When you buck the system around here daddy starts laying down the iron fist. He hates to be challenged or questioned about anything.

Ario and Kaimen are scared to speak up but I'm going to step.

Ario supported me one hundred percent on my decision. He's always done his best to protect me and it would break my heart if he ever found out he didn't protect me from the monster under our roof growing up.

My childhood trauma was the reason I decided it was time to heal from my past.

It was paralyzing my future and I owed it to myself to get unstuck. It was the only thing my father was paying for. He was only footing the bill out of guilt.

I looked myself over in my mirror to make sure my make-up was still flawless. I ruffled my curls with my fingers and touched up my lip gloss. My fresh wash had me feeling like I was walking on air.

My natural beauty was credited to my mother. I didn't favor her but she was just as flawless as I was.

I made the cars wait as I made my way across the street to the thirteen-story building. It was only appropriate that my therapist was on the top floor in the penthouse suite.

For what she was charging I expected nothing less.

The lilac and sandalwood scent seductively danced in the air on the clouds on depression forcing your mind into serene relaxation.

"Mrs. Yarbrough to see Ms. Carruthers," I advised the front desk receptionist.

"Please take a seat. She will be out shortly."

I thumbed through the Essence magazine taking note of the newest fashion trends.

I skimmed through the quiz quickly calculating my numbers to see what my results were.

"I will see you next week," I heard my therapist say.

"Bre?"

I couldn't believe what I was seeing. My brother's wife Brechelle was leaving my therapist's office.

She just got in this family and they're already driving this girl to therapy. I didn't care for her because she comes off as a goody to shoes.

We never really had words because she knows better but something about her is off. I realized I was on to something when I bumped into someone who knew her.

Parelle was not someone you would normally see me hanging with. He was G to the H-E-T-T-O.

I was praying that he really used my card and called me with more information.

Running into him was a sign that she needs to be exposed.

Once I proved that Kaimen's wife was bad for my father's image he would start grooming Ario.

My daddy's hard on Ario but he's the most capable to be his successor even though my dad will never admit to it.

"Oh, hey girl. I didn't know you see Dr. Carruthers," she flashed a fake smile.

"Yeah, this family will drive you crazy if you allow it," I returned the same fake smile.

If she knew like I knew she would have her demented husband here with her.

Kaimen acts like this good guy but nothing is further from the truth. He's evil and the worst one of us all if you ask me.

I've never spent time with Bre but if she knew like I knew she would watch her back. I wonder what she was here talking to the doctor about. Maybe she already knows about the monster she's married to.

"Well, I have to get back to the office before Ario poaches my patients. You enjoy your day."

Her and Kaimen were always throwing shade at my brother. If she keeps on, I'll drag her through the streets of Houston by that non blending lace front.

"Come on in Ms. Yarbrough," Dr. Carruthers motioned for me to come into her office.

I walked in and took my seat on my favorite orange couch.

Her office decor was filled with bright colors that helped to fight off your depression.

"So how is the job search going?" She dived right in.

She gave me that task last week of finding a job to support myself instead of throwing a tantrum with my father whenever I didn't get what I want.

I felt that he owed it to me to run up a check with all that I've been through. It's his fault I'm the way that I am.

"It's not going."

"So, you're going to allow your father to continue to control you with money?"

"What else am I supposed to do? Work?" I turned up my nose at the very thought of clocking in to work for someone.

I was not built for that.

"I mean that's what the rest of us adults have to do," she said writing on her yellow legal pad.

Dr. Carruthers was old school. She had a laptop but she wrote everything down and used one of those old tape recorders. It was weird but she was the best in the city so it works for her.

"I'm not proud of the fact that I allow him to control me with money but after I give him this ultimatum, I don't think I will have this problem much longer."

"What ultimatum?"

"Nothing for you to worry about. Just know I have a plan."

"That's what worries me. I urge you to find your own means of financial stability. You can't keep depending on your father to take care of you. You're an adult Allacia. You're very capable. You have a bachelor's in business that you don't bother to use. Why did you stop doing consulting work?"

"Because I don't like people."

"Seriously?"

Abigail gave me this same rant each time I sat down with her. I pretended to listen knowing I was still going to walk out those doors and do my own thing.

I was paying her to listen to my problems, not fix them. I just needed someone who was under legal obligation not to disclose my deepest darkest secrets.

"Ms. Carruthers, I have an urgent matter to talk to you about."

"You know you're not to interrupt my sessions under any circumstances."

"I understand but this is urgent," she reiterated.

Abigail slammed her pen down and stopped the recording, "I apologize. Please excuse me."

Once she was out of the room, I went over to her desk to see if her notes from Brechelle was there. I knew the chances were slim to none but was also hoping that because she didn't plan on being called out that I would find something on Bre.

I thumbed through the papers.

"OH MY GOD!!" I yelled.

What I read from Dr. Carruthers notes had me shook! I finally had something on Kaimen that would devastate him and bring his entire world down.

I quickly put the papers back like I found them and sat back down. My heart was racing so fast I could barely sit still. If she didn't end this session I was about to. The tea I have is piping hot and burning in my soul!

I just may have just secured my financial stability the good doctor was encouraging me to find.

I'm sure she would pay handsomely to keep her secret buried.

Chapter 7

KAIMEN

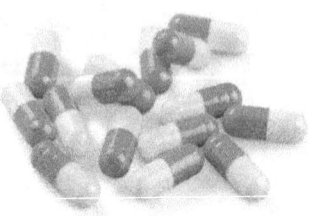

The week went by in a blur. Brechelle still hasn't said anything about an appointment with a fertility specialist. She hasn't been home much but if she thinks working all the time will buy her some time, she is sorely mistaken.

By the time she makes it home I'm asleep and by the time I wake up she's gone. If I didn't know any better, she was avoiding me. I purposely got up earlier this morning to confront her.

"Morning baby," she hooked an arm around my neck.

Bre was lovely. She was the perfect trophy wife. She looked amazing on my arm at dinners, parties, and on magazine covers. We were among the who's who in the medical community. A medical power couple is what they called us.

"Don't morning me. You think you slick coming home late at night and hitting the door before I leave?"

"Being slick? You're being paranoid! It's really too early for this."

"Have you decided on a specialist?"

"Look, I'm looking for the best. That takes time!"

"How much time could it take? We're both doctors and I gave you a list of colleagues of mine that are more than willing to take on our case."

"I don't want your people all in our business. I want to find someone who doesn't know us personally which is hard because you're an OB/GYN!"

"Find someone and I mean quick! I want a child and I'm not going to keep waiting around for you to give me one!"

"What is that supposed to mean?"

"Take it how you want!" I snatched my shirt off the footboard and headed downstairs.

Bre better find her someone else to play with. She's so futile. This girl has been putting off giving me a child for a year now. It's been one excuse after another.

Once I made it back upstairs Bre was already gone. Even though we worked in the same metroplex we drove separate cars to work.

I stop by the homeless shelter before work and helped out. I assist with making breakfast and serving those less fortunate. I was greeted with a long line of residents waiting for food.

A few of the volunteers were sitting freshly washed trays in stacks. The clacking noise alerted those waiting for more trays.

The sour body order that suffocated the air entwined with the alcohol on the breath of many of the residents. It wasn't even eight o'clock yet and they had already hit their bottle and so have I.

I have a couple shots of Jameson to start my morning and end my day. Bre always gave me the side eye when it came to my drinking but I didn't care. I'm grown.

"Man, I know you went through my bag last night while I was sleep!" One resident confronted another.

I waived for security to make their way over to deescalate the situation.

"You better get out of my face while I'm trying to eat Negro!" The other man spat back.

I was thoroughly frustrated with security at this point for not being more proactive in the situation. I couldn't afford to get hurt breaking up a fight so he needed to do his job!

"Hey, go to your separate corners or get banned!"

The men grumbled underneath their breath but obeyed the orders of the security guard.

"Dr. Yarbrough!" Ms. Celeste always welcomed me with open arms.

She was a heavy-set woman with a smile wider than Texas. She wore a wig that wasn't shaped properly and looked a bit brittle but she spruced it up with some sort of oil it appeared. Her full cheeks both adorned dimples that complimented her smile.

Her black flats leaned to the side because her feet were so wide. She had told me on previous occasion that they're her most comfortable shoes. She said she wasn't about to have her feet in bondage while she serviced people.

It wasn't because I was a doctor but because despite my family's notoriety and fortune, I had a desire to help those less fortunate to me.

No, we never grew up in the hood but I loved giving back and helping my people.

"Good morning Ms. Celeste."

"We're just about ready to open the kitchen. Get your cap and apron on. Don't forget your gloves. These people don't need our flanges all over their food," she laughed. "See I know some medical words myself."

"Yes, you do," I joined her in laughter.

Once I had everything on, I took my place on the food line. One after another I handed out plates full of hot breakfast that included eggs, bacon and biscuits. They had the option of coffee or juice that we had sitting out on the table.

After a couple of hours, I noticed Celeste heading my way. She always made sure I go to work on time.

"You better get your butt to work and go deliver some babies!" Ms. Celeste took the spoon from my hand."

"Yes ma'am. I'll see you in the morning."

"Okay baby."

My drive to my office was only about twenty minutes or so. During that time, I normally listened to notes I recorded on my phone about high risk patients I was seeing that day.

I love what I do.

Before I pulled off, I made sure to text Tisha making sure she got the money.

My dad has been messing around with her for almost a year and he thinks she so unproblematic.

I break her off every month to make sure she stays out of the way.

She's not the first and she won't be the last. I hate what my dad is doing to my mom but I just can't stomach him tarnishing his legacy.

I've performed so many abortions over the years on his mistresses.

He insists they all make me their doctor's so he can hook them up with free healthcare.

When that didn't work, he paid them off and still sent them to me.

I was always the one behind the scenes matching up everyone's messes. I hated Ario and

Allacia but our family's future was bigger than any of that. I often cleaned up after those two as well whether they knew it or not.

Ario walks around arrogantly like he's this big-time plastic surgeon when in fact our hospital has paid off more lawsuits that I can count.

If he would quit pushing that garbage up his nose before he operates, he wouldn't be botching surgeries left and right.

I may come off a bit obsessive but my intentions are good. I do this for us all.

I was greeted at my office door by a kid on the run from his mother. His devious grin made me smile as he gave his mom the blues.

I picked him up and handed him back to her.

She mouthed, "Thank you," as she headed back to her seat fussing at him.

"Is this baby April that I delivered six weeks ago?" I asked the patient holding her baby.

"Yes, it is. She's getting so big!"

"Yes, she is! You can't even tell she was underweight! May I?"

"Absolutely."

I picked up the chunky bald baby and held her close to me. She was unbothered as she chewed on her teething ring.

"You not giving her cereal, are you? I saw that post going around talking about some kind of knock out bottle."

"I saw that ridiculous post. Someone gone end up in jail with that mess. No, I've just been breast feeding her. Her body is just responding incredibly."

"Yes, it is."

I held her in the air being sure to dodge the drool falling from her bottom lip.

The women in the waiting room were watching in admiration. It was something about seeing a man with a baby that got their ovaries jumping.

I smiled at them and gave baby April back to her mother who was here for her six-week check-up.

My stride was upbeat as I headed to the back to prepare for the busy day.

BUZZ.

BUZZ.

BUZZ.

I pulled out my phone to see the picture of my beautiful mother plastered on my screen.

I also covered my father's mess because it would destroy my mom if she found out he was being unfaithful.

"Hey mama."

"Hey baby boy. How are you?"

"I'm good mama. How are you?"

"I'm good baby. Just been a little tired."

"Did daddy check you out?"

"Boy stop it! A family full of doctors and a person can't even say their tired in peace," she complained.

I laughed, "Mama you know you're the glue in this family. We would go crazy dealing with each other if it weren't for you."

"You're right about that! All of y'all have your daddy's short temper."

"Not me mama."

"It takes you more to get there but it's there son. I was just calling to tell you to have a blessed day baby. I love you."

"I love you too mama."

"Okay, don't forget about family dinner Sunday."

"How can I mom? Dad will send one of the security team to my house if I'm late," I laughed.

"You're right about that one. Well I gotta go. Love you baby!"

My mother called all her kids in the morning to set the pace for their day. She told us she loved us and encouraged us to be the best version of ourselves daily.

We're grown but my mother still believes in the power a mother has to make or break their child's day.

I'm not sure why she called them other demon spawn of hers because they would find a way to sow seeds of discord despite her positive affirmations.

"Good morning Dr. Yarbrough," Senovia sang.

"How is my favorite nurse?"

"I'm good. I would be better if them bad kids would stick to their sleep schedule," she whined.

"Leave my babies alone."

"Your babies better leave me alone!"

"Ms. Whitley is in room number one."

I rolled my eyes, " Did she take a bath this time?"

"How would I know? You're definitely about to find out," she laughed pointing to the chart outside her door.

I flipped the indicator above her door to the red one letting the staff know which room I was in.

I wouldn't check her until Nadia came back in the room. Until then I would catch up with Ms. Whitley and pray she washed up this go round.

She was here every couple of months because her so called husband burned her. I personally don't think she's married because out of eight pregnancies I've never seen him. Not even once.

Yet here she was again. I wonder if she's pregnant or burning this time. My money would be on the STD if I had to take a wild guess.

"Ms. Whitley you're back to see me, huh?"

"Yeah Doc. I think I'm pregnant again but it burns when I pee so I don't think my pregnancy test will be accurate."

I was sighing on the inside. It was about to smell like hot tuna fish simmered in infection.

"Well, I'll step out so you can get undressed and put on a gown," she took it from me.

"My panties too?"

"Ms. Whitley, this is not your first rodeo. You know you must get completely undressed. Are you okay?"

"Yeah, just tired. My kids wearing me out. I pray it's just another disease and not another baby."

"Well, get changed and we'll figure it out," I placed a hand on her back to assure her.

I felt bad for Ms. Whitley. She didn't keep coming up pregnant due to negligence. She was unusually fertile.

At this point she should just opt for celibacy to be on the safe side.

"Ms. Whitley I can let you know before you leave if your pregnant. The other tests the nurse will have to call you about tomorrow. You know you're extremely fertile. You must accept some level of responsibility for your body. If the kids you have are wearing you out then at least use protection. I have you on the Depo Shot but that doesn't protect you from disease. If you get something you can't get rid of who's going to raise your babies? Do you trust your family to do right by them?" I challenged her.

"You're right Dr. K. I promise this the last time. When I come for my follow-up, I'm going to be different. Watch."

"I'm holding you to it."

"Here are the results for her pregnancy test," my nurse walked in handing me her paperwork.

"You're not pregnant!" I smiled.

"Thank you Jeeessusss!" She exhaled.

"Well, the nurse will call you tomorrow to let you know the results of the rest of your labs."

******

"What's the play for lunch?" Senovia interrupted me updating a few of my patient charts.

"I'm not sure if I want a salad or something heavier," I answered not looking up from my paperwork.

"I brought in some left-over homemade lasagna and garlic bread."

"My favorite," I chimed finally lifting my eyes.

"Yes, I know. Take a break from that paperwork and come and eat."

"Dr. Kaimen your wife is on line one," my receptionist came through over the phone intercom.

"Thank you. Senovia, I will meet you in the break room. This shouldn't be long," I assured her.

"Okay, I'll get everything reheated."

"Afternoon Bre," I spoke dryly into the receiver.

"I found a specialist babe!"

"Great! When do we go in? I can clear my schedule whenever you need me to."

"I'm glad you said that because we can meet with her later today. What time is your last appointment?"

"Around three thirty."

"Great, her office normally closes at four but she will wait for us today. I told her how anxious we are to get the ball rolling. Kaimen, I don't want you to get your hopes up to high. Do you think you will be open to adoption?"

"Absolutely not! Ario already berates me for being and OB/GYN! I refuse to have him disrespecting me because we have to adopt a child for failure of having our own! This will work. Trust me."

Bre was silent on the other end of the phone but I didn't care. The only thing that would make our image even better would be kids. One of the benefits of going the fertility route is being able to choose what sex our baby is. Our son will be born first then our daughter. If we can have twins our branding would be limitless.

"Senovia, I need you to see if Dr. Sanchez can see my last appointment of the day. I need to step out for an emergency appointment."

"Is everything okay?"

"Yes, nothing to worry yourself about. I will be back in the office in the morning. We can still have lunch though," I smiled.

Joy filled me like sunshine as I took my seat in front of Senovia.

"You must've really got some good news to be smiling like that."

"When your life has been in such chaos you learn to appreciate the calm days."

"I hear you."

Senovia and I made small talk the remainder of our lunch break. The remainder of my day flew by. I'm guessing it was from the excitement of Bre finally coming through with a specialist.

I arrived at the destination Bre gave me. It was weird. I'm familiar with all of the doctors in my city and I've never known one to be in the area Bre's specialist is in. It's like she popped up out of no where and I'm not comfortable with that. For now, I will keep my reservations to myself.

A knot formed in my abdomen as I fought against my suspicions.

I took note of the name and credentials on the door at I walked in.

"You found it," Bre ran into my arms forcing an embrace.

The receptionist gave us the side eyes. The office smelled of new paint and plastic. Even to be a new office it was just to clean. It appeared as if no one had been in the building other than the receptionist and us.

"Mr. and Mrs. Yarbrough to see Dr. Green," Bre's eyes sparkled with excitement.

I smiled seeing that she was onboard with making our dream a reality.

"You can come back. Dr. Green will see you now," a short Caucasian girl with a blonde bob smiled as she escorted us back.

"Hello, I'm Dr. Green," a tall thin woman who favored Tyra Banks extended her hand.

"Dr. Yarbrough and Dr. Yarbrough," Bre laughed nervously.

"Well, I guess I won't have to put anything in laymen's terms on our journey," she joined Bre in laughter.

I quite frankly was over the niceties. I was ready to get down to business. I want to know how she planned to address our fertility concerns head on.

"Mr. Yarbrough, you look like you're ready to get down to it. Please take a seat. I'm still building my clientele. I'm new to the area but my credentials and accolades speak for themselves. I was amazed that your wife trusted me with her journey. We'll get some labs and specimens on you both and once I have results, we can formulate a plan. Today I want to hear your concerns and desires for conception."

Bre looked at me.

"What?" I said.

"You've been very vocal about wanting to conceive. Now is your time to shine Dr. Yarbrough," she sat up straight trying to appear extra alert.

"Dr. Green, we've been trying for over a year to conceive to no avail. I'm an OB/GYN so I'm able to recognize possible issues when it comes to conception. I do like the fact that your practice is new so that means you will be completely devoted to us during this process."

"I have a few clients but you are correct, the majority of my time will be devoted to your case. What about you Mrs. Yarbrough?"

"It's Dr. and I just want to find out what's wrong so we can fix it."

"You both are straightforward. I like that. Here are the orders for your labs," she handed my wife two orders.

"When do we need to have them completed?" I asked.

"As soon as possible," Dr. Green said. "You also need to make another appointment so we can get you in to get a specimen of your sperm."

"Okay, I can take care of it today."

"Great! When I get results, we'll develop a plan of action to get you both pregnant."

"Thank you for your time!"

I was hopeful as I stopped by the front desk to retrieve my specimen cup. I've already had my sperm checked but if she wants a fresh sample I will gladly oblige.

"You can come this way Dr. Yarbrough," the nurse smiled. "If you need your wife's help she can come as well."

"No, I should be fine."

Brechelle was clearly offended but I just wanted to get this done and over with.

"Okay, I'll wait for you here."

"No need. I have an errand to run after I leave here. I don't want to hold up baby," I kissed her and followed the nurse back.

Chapter 8

ARIO

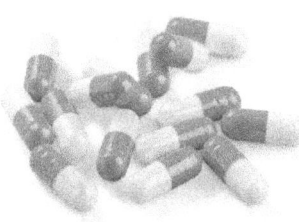

"You've been avoiding me because you know you're foul!" Bre spoke through clenched teeth as she entered my office.

"I haven't seen you because I've been busy with cases unlike you. You haven't even been in this office to notice if I was here or not. What have you been running in and out of this office doing?"

"Mind your business."

"Nah, you come in here with all of that yappin'. Where you been Bre?"

"Leave it alone."

"You the one started it."

"No, let's talk about that comment you made when you and Kaimen were arguing at the house!"

"Girl, that's so old."

"It's not old! You were wrong for throwing me under the bus! Why would you do me like that?"

"You know why," I smiled at her.

"Kaimen should've broke your nose," she scoffed.

"These million-dollar hands aren't for fighting. I make enough money to have your husband touched if I wanted to."

"Watch your mouth!"

"Or what?" I antagonized her.

"Your appointment is here," the receptionist interrupted us.

"Send them in," we replied in unison.

We took our seats on the same side of the conference table. Bre could save all the cap for someone who cared. We both know what it is.

"Welcome Phyllis. It's a pleasure to meet you. What brings you to our office?" I asked her.

"Well...I'm a hermaphrodite and I want to choose a genital," she pulled her ball cap lower to cover her face.

"You have nothing to be ashamed of," Bre consoled her. "Why did you wait so long?"

"Initially, my parents wanted me to get older to see which sex I gravitated to. What they failed to realize was the older I got the more expensive the procedure would be. Once I was able to decide, they could no longer afford it. I've worked two jobs for the past five years to be able to afford my procedure. I'm ready to move forward with my life."

"Phyllis, we admire your courage. What sex did you decide on?" I asked.

"I'm a woman. I cover up like this because I'm ashamed of my body. I'm ready to get this done so I can blossom and be free," she smiled for the first time since coming into the conference room.

"Well, let us walk you out so the nurse can get you scheduled for some labs and radiology procedures. Once we have the results, we'll call you back in with our plan of action," Bre explained.

"Thank you both so much!"

"You're quite welcome," I said.

Bre was the one who specialized in gender reassignment. I wasn't getting into all of that. It was too emotionally draining for me. She asked me to assist with more of the cosmetic aspect. She wants the incisions seamless after they heal.

I'm the best to ever do it. I've been published in medical magazines so many times I've lost count. My dad is the only one who's been published more than me.

Kaimen has some for his advancement in fetal medicine. Everyone in the U.S. knows it's all about the cut and tuck these days.

Social media has branded this image of perfection that has not only consumed women but men as well.

Men come in just as much as women these days for pec enhancements and anything else they believe will make them more desirable.

Everyone wants to be wanted. It's not just by one person either. People wants the world to desire them. Those likes, hearts and comments have become their daily affirmation of worth.

It's sad but I've built a profitable practice on it. The only reason I haven't separated from my father's lil' metroplex is because I got next on the throne.

I've already been talking to some board members and they are tired of my father's controlling attitude.

Kaimen thinks he will inherit my dad's legacy but nothing could be further from the truth. He's weak and his constant need for validation is sickening.

I'm tired of hearing, "You're such an innovator like you father."

I'm an innovator like myself! I'm the future and my father is the past.

"So, what do you think?" Bre asked.

"About what?"

"Phyllis! Isn't she amazing! This will be groundbreaking to perform this procedure on someone so old."

"You are way too excited about this mediocre procedure. I have something better for you to get excited about," I stepped closer to Bre.

I watched her breathing become labored as I invaded her space.

I was so close our lips nearly touched.

"Mrs. Yar-"

Bre and I weren't doing anything wrong but we both looked guilty.

"Who let you back here Senovia?" Bre screamed.

"Your husband spoke to your staff and advised them to let me back whenever I come over."

"He what?"

"I thought he told you both. My apologies. He sent over some documents he said couldn't wait."

Bre snatched the envelope from Senovia. Senovia's jawline was clenched so tight I could see the outline of her jawbone and some teeth.

"What are you still standing there for? You can leave!"

Senovia rolled her eyes and took her leave.

"Are you happy? You know she's going to run back to Kaimen and tell him what she saw!"

"What did she see Bre?"

"You all in my face! I told you that we are done. Kaimen and I are in a better place and we're working on having a baby."

"He has a low sperm count so you won't get pregnant. Besides, if you wanted a baby, I would've given you one a long time ago."

"I will never go that far with you. I have enough to feel guilty about. Besides, you discuss me."

"Girl please. I far from disgust you and we both know that. I'll leave you here to ponder your own lies.

I left her standing there to lie to herself. We both know she says this every month and each month she ends up back in my bed.

To be honest I wasn't the least bit attracted to Bre. I only entertained her because she was my brother's wife and I despised him.

I have so many videos of Bre and I together that I plan on shattering him with.

If I'm nothing else, I'm a patient man.

My ultimate goal is to obliterate Kaimen emotionally, physically and mentally. I want to watch him deteriorate until he's only a shell of his former self.

I looked at my watch and it was time for me to go to the E.R. for my shift tonight.

I was dreading being on call with him tonight in the E.R. It was my father's way of punishing us.

"Dr. Yarbrough we have to be in full P.P.E. we may have a MRSA exposure. It's not confirmed yet but we're being proactive. They've already quarantined the other side over there," she pointed.

"Wonderful," I sighed.

I wasn't tripping because they normally only called me in when they needed me to keep a person's body the way they remember.

If they called me for anything other than that they know it's up there. All night I'm being a jerk. They run Kaimen like an errand boy because he allows it. He's such a people pleaser.

He's only supposed to deal with coochies and babies and he be doing everything in between in this E.R.

"UUUHHHHH," a lady screeched as she was wheeled in by the paramedics.

Brooke was a familiar paramedic that worked our hospital and I could tell she was over this lady's theatrics.

"What is that smell?" I asked.

"Her," Brooke scoffed handing me the report.

From what I was reading she had a small tear on her rectum that she left untreated and it smells like it's infected.

"Kaimen, bro you up," I laughed stuffing the chart in his arms.

"Ah nah. I'm good. I'm on baby duty tonight."

"You both will."

We spun around at the sound of my dad's voice.

"Take her to the side that's quarantined," he instructed the nurses.

"Help me please!"

The lady continued to cry.

"Okay ma'am. We need you relax a bit. We're going to give you something for the pain," I nodded to the nurse.

The lady was still uncomfortable but the pain was a bit more bearable.

The visor didn't do any justice. She opened her legs and it smelled like a unkept slaughterhouse.

"Oh God," Kaimen mumbled trying not to vomit.

"You better not!"

"What's going on with her?" He struggled to ask.

"I think some of this infected tissue is dead. We're going to have to cut this out of her before it kills her. I know you've seen worse delivering babies."

"Not like this," he panted.

We both doubled on protective gear and did our best to give this woman some relief.

"Did you feel her stomach? It's really hard. I think she's constricted."

"Don't!"

Before I could stop him Kaimen pressed on her stomach. Flesh and tissue went everywhere. The nurses helping us tossed their professionalism to the side and bolted.

Gunk was on the ceiling, equipment, filled my both my shoes, and was plastered on Kaimen's goggles.

The lady's vitals were stable but she was passed out. I think she finally got some relief. Kaimen and I spent hours repairing her rectum.

I made my dad send a sanitation team to try and clean some of the mess up. I just had to get her patched up enough so she could go into surgery.

I can do anything but I don't get paid to do this. These million dollars hands don't belong elbows deep in dead rectum tissue.

I tossed my three-hundred-dollar shoes away without hesitation. I went home in some hospital slippers, scrubs, and a humble spirit. Don't nothing humble you like working in the E.R.

"Get home safe," Kaimen said.

"Same to you."

Sometimes I wished I had a better relationship with my brother but then he would do something stupid to remind me why I don't deal with him.

There wasn't just one thing that happened. It's been a lifetime of unfortunate events that have landed us on opposite sides of the line drawn in the sand.

One thing I learned quickly with Kaimen was that blood don't make you family.

Chapter 9

ALLACIA

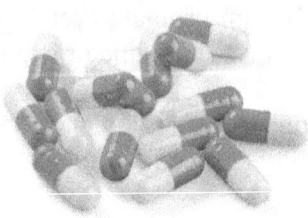

I slipped my heels off so my landlord wouldn't hear me coming up the walkway. The rough gravel caused the bottom of my feet to tingle but I had to do what I had to do. I was fuming that I had to resort to such measures all because my dad cut me off.

"I thought I saw you pull up," Lenora folded her arms across her perfectly aligned implants.

I knew my rent paid for that customized body she flaunted around our complex. She owned all ten units and I was jealous.

Lenora bragged all the time how she took the money her dad gave her at graduation and invested in this property. She bought it dirt cheap and remolded everything. She quadrupled her investment and brought other business in the neighborhood which increased her property value even more.

"Yes, I had to take these shoes off girl. You know how these red bottoms do," I attempted to joke.

"Maybe you should sell a few pair so you can pay your rent up," she snarled flipping her jet-black weave.

Everything about this chick was fake except for her fat bank account. She was definitely getting to the money. If she wasn't my nemesis, I could've got some pointers from her.

"My dad is going to give me the money to pay it up. I've been busy so I haven't had the time to pick it up."

"I remember when my dad use to pay my rent while I was in college but I've been independent since. I suppose people are simply different," she shrugged. "I'll tell you what. You can just go get it now so I don't have to post this eviction notice on your door," she waived the paper in my face.

I wanted to slap her hand and face simultaneously but I kept is classy.

"You don't have to do that. I can go and get the money from him now," I lied to her.

The truth was I was cut off and the only way I could break my dad was blackmailing him for real.

I turned on my heels and made my way back to my car. I wasn't leaving without a check in my hand.

On the entire drive there I could only think about trying to come up with a way to support myself. I know that my dad was trying to use tough love to get me on track but I don't want that. I want him to keep taking care of me. I don't know how to take care of myself on the level that he has all my life.

I waived to the security guard Frank who was posted at the gate. He was senile and often let people in who wasn't supposed to get through. He's been with my dad so long he just didn't have the heart to fire or replace him.

I pulled my car around to the circle drive to the front double doors.

I inhaled and exhaled deeply as I gripped my steering wheel. My palms were already sweating.

I grabbed my purse and headed inside.

"Where is my dad?" I asked one of the servants.

"He's in his study."

"Thanks!"

I marched down the hall with purpose. They were cleaning so disinfectant flooded my nostrils. I loved the smell of bleach and Mr. Clean.

I didn't bother to knock.

"Daddy, I need to talk to you!"

He gently removed his glasses from his face and placed the tip in his mouth.

"So, you think you just gone barge in here and disrupt what I'm doing to demand something of me?" He waived his glasses around as if they were a part of his props.

"Look, it you don't start back paying my bills I'm going to tell mama about what happened when I was ten! That's the reason I've been struggling so to get my crap together! I'm still in therapy!"

"I know. I'm paying for it! Don't come in here demanding nothing from me! People endure tragedy every day! Stop using it as a crutch Allacia and get over it!"

"Get over it? Get over it? Let's see if mommy gets over it!" I turned and ran right into my mother.

My heart almost leaped out of my chest cavity. I only wanted my dad to know I was serious. I wasn't prepared to tell her. Was I?

"What is going on here?"

Dad and I both were silent as mice.

"I said what's going on?" She yelled. What is she talking about Cliff? What happened to her at ten? What did you do to her?" Tears filled my mama's eyes and her hands started to tremble.

"No mama, it's not what you think."

"Well, somebody better say something!" She collapsed to the floor.

"Darcy!" My dad ran over to my mama who was unresponsive."

"Daddy, save her," I yelled frantically.

Every nerve ending in my body was on fire. I watched in daze as my dad administered CPR.

"Alli call 911!" He yelled snapping me back to reality.

I did as he asked.

"This is why I didn't tell her! Her heart is bad! We've been waiting for a time to tell you all but you're all so selfish! Always fighting!" He stopped compressions to place his mouth on my mother's to exhale oxygen into her body.

I watched her chest expand and prayed she would be okay. I didn't know she was that sick.

Guilt was creeping over me like cold ice water in the pit of my stomach.

"We can take it from here Dr. Yarbrough," the paramedic scooted in front of my dad who sat there helpless. It was as if he knew something no one in the room did.

My dad rode in the ambulance and I followed in my car. I sent a group text to my brothers to meet me at the hospital because mom collapsed.

I didn't tell them why. Kaimen would eat me alive if he knew about what just happened. We hated each other!

Despite my dad owning the hospital they made us stay in the waiting area. My dad was broken. I've never seen him like this.

"Dad, I'm-"

"Don't you dare!"

I immediately closed my mouth and waited for Ario to arrive. Both of my brothers came running through the double glass doors and I knew better than to think they rode together.

"What happened?" Kaimen asked.

"Ask your sister," my dad cut his eyes at me.

"What happened Alli?"

"I was arguing with daddy and mom walked in and started asking questions. Next thing I knew she collapsed. Dad said her heart was worse than they led on."

"What were y'all arguing about?" Kaimen snarled.

"What do you think?" I retorted.

I was fully prepared to have him admitted to this hospital for a sliced throat if he tried me.

******

`Dr. Salmon came out with a grim look on his face.

"We did all we could but your wife's heart was beyond repair.

"Noooo," my dad let out a wail that would haunt me until the day I died. " She left here thinking I did something I didn't. She left here without me telling her the truth," he collapsed to the floor.

He was consumed with grief.

I watched life leave him and he collapsed right on the floor.

"Get me a crash cart! Now!" Dr. Salmon called out to one of the nurses.

It was like a horrible nightmare that kept repeating itself except this time it was my dad.

I know we had our issues but I can't live my life without this man! He drives me crazy but he is my rock!

"Code Stroke ER, Code Stroke ER, Code Stroke ER," the operator announced overhead.

A few security guards walked up and stood near us.

If they knew my brothers like I did then they would know this was a great idea.

"Dad!" Kaimen screamed.

Ario was next to Dr. Salmon trying to assist him even though he told him to stay back. He's also Ario's godfather so his words were falling on deaf ears at the moment.

They finally pulled all three of us back so the rest of the team could load my dad on the stretcher and get him back into the E.R.

"Are you going to tell me what really happened?" Kaimen inquired.

His beady eyes were penetrating my being as if he were trying to will the answers out of me.

"I told you."

"Nah, you talked around it. All I know is I got a dead mama and probably a soon to be daddy because of something you did," he snapped walking upon me.

"Chill," Ario got between us making sure Kaimen didn't put his hands on me.

"Allacia, what happened?" Ario questioned me.

"Me and dad was arguing about him not paying my bills and mom walked in. She told us to stop but you know how dad and I go at it. She got overwhelmed and collapsed. That's when dad told me that they had been trying to tell us at family dinner for some time now that mom's heart was about to give out on her."

Kaimen gave me the side eye which meant he wasn't satisfied with my answer.

I didn't care because there was no way I was about to tell them I was the reason mama fell dead.

"All you do is lie," Kaimen pushed. "What were y'all really arguing about?"

"You know what we ALWAYS argue about!" I spat daring him to keep pushing me.

Me, him and daddy know exactly why we always go at it! Ario and mama are the only ones still in the dark.

Kaimen is a snake. Always slithering around in places he has no business being.

"Call me when y'all hear something. I can't take this waiting around," I snatched up my purse and headed towards the exit.

The hot Texas heat was symbolic of the hell I was living in now.

I jumped on forty-five north and made my way home.

"Did you get my money?" Lenora met me at the end of the sidewalk.

I wasn't in the mood for her attitude. My mama just died and my daddy may be on his way to join her for all I knew.

"My mama just died Lenora. I went over there to ask my dad for the money and she collapsed right in front of me," a single tear escaped my eye.

I wasn't the crying type which was why I was so bitter. The tears rolled back instead of out in turn they stained my soul.

"Cry me a river. People will make up any lie to avoid paying their bills. You should be ashamed of yourself lying like that!"

"Who are you that I have to lie?"

I dropped my purse and heels on the ground and charged at Lenora.

I grabbed a handful of her weave and wrapped it around my hand.

"Let me go!" She screamed.

Despite my blurred vision I could see people running out of their apartments and taking front row seats on the balcony.

I was doing what everyone else has been wanting to do for years down.

"You stupid trick!" I brought my foot down across her face.

In the back of my mind I already knew I might as well pack up my condo and move back to my daddy house.

We had the best lawyer money could buy so I wasn't worried about this assault charge I was about to take.

"Somebody help me!" her voice cracked as she pleaded for the spectators to help her.

I dropped the weight of my body on her and wrapped my hands around her throat. I could feel my temples throbbing as her tongue hung out of her mouth.

"Okay, that's enough," I heard a baritone voice grunt in my ear.

I gave one final kick to Lenora's face. The crimson blood from her bottom lip rendered me the satisfaction I deserved.

"Ario! Come to my house ASAP! I need you!" I demanded while trying to catch my breath.

"What's wrong?!"

I could hear the panic in his voice.

"I'll explain when you get here. Get a moving truck over here like yesterday!" I said ending the call.

If no one came to my rescue I knew I could count on Ario.

He was the only person I knew really loved me now that my mother was gone.

Chapter 10

ALLACIA

Two Weeks Later

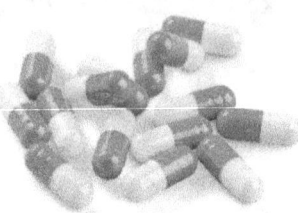

"Where is dad?" Ario nervously paced back and forth.

He didn't need surgery or anything for his stroke but it took him a couple of weeks to get back on his feet.

We dared not have mom's funeral without him being there.

My dad had a family burial plot built when he designed the estate layout. It looked as if it was open to the public as nice as it was. Some people thought it was weird and others admired the ingenuity.

My dad always wanted us close ever after death. He said if he or mom passed that he wanted us to be able to come and sit and talk with them even though they were long gone.

We all stayed at the big house to be close to dad but he managed to sneak out. After stomping Lenora out, I had no choice but to move back on the estate. My father couldn't stand the site of me so I stayed with Ario for the time being.

We had no idea where daddy was.

Kaimen was on his phone but couldn't manage to locate my dad. He turned his phone off so we couldn't track him.

"I think I know where he is," Ario bit down on his bottom lip as he dialed a number on his phone.

I watched him walk around in a circle as he mumbled to someone on the other end of the call.

"He's in surgery," he finally said hanging up the phone. "He got called in on a special case. They said they didn't want to bother him with everything going on but dad insisted if they needed him not to hesitate to call him in. I'm going to go and get him."

"What?! Are they stupid? That man just had a stroke and they're still calling him? Ario, let Kaimen go. You and daddy like oil and water and I don't want y'all arguing. It'll just make it harder to get him here. People are going to start arriving soon so we need to get him here and dressed within the next hour and a half."

"Okay," he didn't put up a fight for the first time ever.

"I'll be right back with him," Kaimen assured us. "Bre baby are you coming with me?"

"No, I better stay here just in case the guest start to arrive I can help Alli."

"Okay, bet. I'll be right back y'all."

It was the first time in a long time that we were all amicable towards one another.

"Bre let's get all of the flower arrangements set. After that we can make sure the staff has all the food mama requested."

"Whatever you need me to do Sis," she smiled embracing me.

Mama had everything planned out the way she wanted it. She picked out her casket, flower arrangements, and coordinated the menu for her repass. She was such a classy lady even in death.

My mother's service was set-up more like a gala than a funeral service.

While nitpicking with the staff about the food in the kitchen I saw Ario and Bre disappear into one of the rooms.

"Excuse me," I told Esmerelda, my mother's kitchen staff coordinator.

I kicked my heels off near the couch in the living room so they wouldn't hear me coming. After catching a glimpse of her confession to Dr. Carruthers about sleeping with Ario I've been giving her the side eye.

I'm not sure how long or if they're still messing around but she was gone have to pay me to keep my mouth closed.

Personally, I could care less that she was cheating on Kaimen. Good for her to get her something on the side. I was just going to blackmail her so I can pay my bills.

I creeped up to the door but could only hear muffled sounds. I headed into the adjoining room next door. They were in my dad's office and there was a sitting room with a door I could slip in to eavesdrop.

I pulled my phone out to record whatever I found as evidence.

I grabbed the hook of the door handle and gently pulled it down so that it wouldn't make a sound.

I stuck my camera through the small opening.

"Ario now is not the time. We could get caught. Your sister running around here somewhere."

I was watching them on my phone slob each other down like we weren't about to bury my mama.

That's why she really didn't want to go with her husband.

Ario positioned himself on my father's mahogany desk. I watched Bre disappear in front of him and it didn't take a genius to figure out what she was doing.

"Ms. Yarbrough? Esmeralda called out to me causing me to jump.

I could hear Ario and Bre scuffling around on the other side of the door.

"Yes. What can I do for you?"

"The guests are arriving. I couldn't find any of you so I had them wait in the sitting room. I wasn't sure if you wanted them to view the body yet or not."

"Thank you but not yet. You did right. I need to look over my mother once more before allowing the rest of her friends to view her one last time."

Once Esmerlda disappeared I pulled out my phone.

"Hey boo. Can you come to my mama funeral? I'm sorry for asking you last minute."

I smiled as my special guest agreed to my last-minute invitation.

My mother's body was set-up in the west wing of my father's mansion. Bre and I attended to the flower arrangements where we would hold the repass but I was scared to go in the room where my mama's body was.

This would be the last time I saw her.

My feet felt as if they were sinking in quicksand as I walked towards the room. The large clear vases filled with long white stem roses welcomed me.

The attendants were positioned where we had instructed them and were patiently waiting for the guest to arrive.

They nodded sympathetically as I made my way down the aisle. The clear chairs each had a copy of my mother's obituary. We used the professional picture she had taken for her gala marketing materials.

She was gorgeous. Her smiled beamed and offered hope even through a picture.

I picked up one of the programs and traced my mother's smile with my finger. One of my tears fell and soaked through slightly fading her picture.

I felt as if my stomach was about to fall through my uterus.

The best part of me was lying in a casket and I had no idea who I would become without my mother being my voice of reason. She always pulled me back from the ledge of self-destruction and I was terrified that there was no longer anyone to keep me at bay.

I felt like my hope died with her.

"I'm sorry mama," I brushed her curls back from her face.

Her stylist insisted on doing her hair and not one curl was out of place.

My mother's beauty was frozen in time and she appeared to be only sleeping.

"I know I disappointed you so much but you never gave up on me. You always told me even if I didn't want to be a doctor you were confident I could be anything I set my mind too."

"Kaimen has dad upstairs getting dressed," Ario interrupted my conversation with my mother.

"What are you doing messing with that girl?" I blurted out.

"Mind your business Alley," he snapped.

"I'm just saying. You know I could care less but dad don't need any more drama from us right now. He needs us more than ever."

"I got this. Your brother act like he's untouchable so I'm touching his wife soul," he laughed.

"This is not a game Ario!"

"Girl, you hate that nigga just as much as I do so stop it!" He popped his lapels and took his seat on the front row.

I rolled my eyes and took my seat next to him.

The April showers had it raining cats and dogs outside. You could hear the rain beating against the side of the windows.

It didn't stop people from showing up to see my mother off. I started to worry if we would have enough space for everyone.

Kaimen came in escorting dad. My dad was walking like his legs were wet spaghetti noodles. Pain was twisted all in his face. To know my selfishness could've caused all of this had my heart forcing its way up my esophagus.

Ario's bottom lip began to tremble as his tears tormented him. My mother babied him the most. It's the reason I feel he was an overgrown man-child who refused to mature in life.

I didn't have room to talk though. My tantrum caused my mother to leave this earth. My father can't stand the sight of me.

Kaimen's face was like stone. My eyes fell to Brielle's hand wrapped in his. When I looked up her eyes met mine.

I pursed my lips to the side letting her know I was on to her. Triflin'.

I smiled when Parelle walked in. Brechelle had my family twisted in the game if she thinks we're going to put our family's legacy at risk for her.

I motioned for him to come closer to sit next to me.

I was relieved he dressed for the occasion and actually looked very dapper.

"I'm glad I could be here for you boo," he kissed me on the cheek.

Brechelle's face was frozen in terror when she saw him.

He looked back and smiled at her giving a friendly wave.

This should be interesting. I know this is my mama's funeral but this trick don't get a pass. I'm applying all pressure until she breaks.

******

The funeral went on for a grueling three hours. Having to embrace strangers, repeatedly go down memory lane and smile when I wanted to scream was to much.

I notice my dad leaving so I decided to follow him to make sure he was okay.

I saw him hcading towards the side entrance to leave so I hurried behind him. I wasn't sure where he was going but we have enough servants to go retrieve whatever he needs.

"Daddy where are you going?" I called to him.

He ignored me and got in his car. I watched him until his taillights were all that I could see until it was dark.

I sprinted back inside to tell Ario.

"What's wrong?" Kaimen asked.

Just looking at him made my stomach turn but I was worried about daddy.

"Daddy just got in his car and left. Do you know where he went? We still have a lot of guest here."

"I don't know but I'm about to find out," he said pulling out his phone. "Daddy? Dad, where are you going?"

I paced back and forth biting on my nails waiting for Kaimen to fill me in.

"He said he's going back to the hospital!"

Something was telling me that was a lie.

"What?! He can't do that! Kaimen call them before he kills someone. He's in no head space to operate!"

"I know! I'm on it. Tell Bre I'll be back. I'm going to the hospital."

"Okay."

Hopefully, she wasn't on top of Ario. Triflin'.

Chapter 11

KAIMEN

Two weeks later

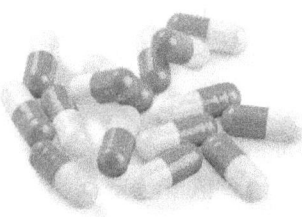

I sucked in air and blew it out as I watched my lungs expand. I focused on imaging the air being pushed down to my toes and coming back up when I exhaled. I grabbed my briefcase and walked into my office.

"What are you doing back so soon?" Senovia scolded me.

"I was going crazy at home. I had to get out of the house. I have patients who need me anyways," I flashed a crooked smile.

"Did you go to the shelter before coming here?"

"No, I wanted to but I just want to take it slow ya' know."

"Yeah. How about I meet you there in the morning?"

"You don't have to do that."

"I want to," her smile encouraged my heart.

Dad has been giving us hell about keeping him out of surgery. Ario and I have been taking turns watching him. We can only do so much now we're back at our practices.

Dad insists that being at the hospital helps takes his mind off losing my mother. We're all missing her like crazy and I think I understand how he feels. I had to do the same thing today.

Somehow just walking into this office lifted the bricks from my chest just a bit. My mother was our peace and I missed her morning calls reminding me how awesome I am.

We stopped doing Sunday dinners because dad just hasn't been up to it. We're already trying to keep him from performing surgeries so we didn't want to press the issue.

We didn't want to be around each other like that anyway. We were just doing that for mama.

Bre wasn't much of a cook but we've been managing. Worst case scenario we would go to the big house for dinner. The staff still cooked even though most of the time my dad didn't eat.

I knew because Esmerelda told me. I had her monitoring his eating habits.

I stuck my hand up so many vaginas that the day seemed to just fly by. My patients missed me and I missed them just as much.

"Your last appointment is here," Senovia laughed.

"What?"

"It's Ms. Whitley."

"You know what? I'm even happy to see her today," I joined her in laughter.

"Mr. Yarbrough! I don't need to see you. My cat clean and ain't no baby in there," she blurted out while walking down the hall. "I got a degree as a medical assistant!" She shoved the paper in my face.

"No way!" I wrapped my arms around her twirling her in the air. "I'm so proud of you!"

"I did it! I did it! I'm about to give my babies the life they deserve Dr. Kaimen!"

I could feel her warm tears on my neck.

"You never put me down when I would come in here. You always encouraged me to do better and that's just what I did," she continued. "Next is nursing!"

"You can do anything you want Ms. Whitley," I wiped the tears from my eyes.

"And don't bill my insurance. I ain't got time for no bill," she laughed.

"How about this?" I pulled my wallet out and handed her five one-hundred-dollar bills.

"What's this for?"

"A graduation present."

"Dr. Kaimen you gone make a baby thug cry," she extended her arms to take the money from my hands.

"You deserve it. Now go kiss those babies for me."

"I sure will."

"That was so sweet of you," Senovia was leaning on the wall with a look of admiration on her face.

"She deserved it."

"She did. We still on for dinner tonight?"

"Yes, we are. Let's shut things down so we can get out of here."

****

"Where have you been?" Bre blew her top.

She had every right to be upset with me. I enjoyed being with Senovia so much I lost track of time.

"I've been calling and texting you but I guess you were too busy to check in with your wife! Have you lost your ever-loving mind? That's what we're doing now? Not answering phones when the other calls? You sholl right nigga! It's almost midnight!"

"Can I speak now?"

"Sure! I know you got your lie locked and loaded my nigga!" I could see the veins bulging from her neck she was screaming so hard.

"I took my staff out to dinner. They held everything down for me for two weeks and I just wanted to do something nice for them. I meant to call you but the day was so hectic. I was so behind we were seeing patients back to back to catch up. I wasn't thinking. I took them straight to eat. Every time I pulled my phone out, I forgot."

"You forgot? Yeah aight."

"Bre, give me a break! My mama just died. I'm just trying get a hold back on my life without her in it. I forgot! I apologized but that's all I got for you right now."

I watched her face soften.

"I'm sorry babe. I'm being selfish. I was just worried. You know your dad is taking this hard and y'all are having to watch him. I was worried you went off the deep end to. If anything happened to you, I would lose my mind."

"You won't ever lose me Bre. You're my wife and I love you. If you died, I think I'd try to raise you from the dead woman or freeze your body until they approved human trials for clones."

"Don't include me in the trial. You gotta save my body until they got it right," she laughed nudging me in my side.

"I got you babe and I'm sorry too."

"Let's go work on this baby," she flicked her tongue lodging it in the roof of her mouth.

"Yes, lets."

Chapter 12

BRECHELLE

This fertility appointment came just in time. Kaimen has been down lately with the death of his mom. I suppose that's the reason he's been so distant lately. I can't lose this man. Kaimen is the best thing to ever happen to me. I was already a boss. I mean I brought a table to the table. I love and need him as a person. I crave this man. His scent is intoxicating to me. I'm not talking about cologne either. I'm talking about that smell when my face is nestled in his neck as his whispers in my ears everything I've ever wanted to hear a man say.

Kaimen was my safety net. He allowed me to be me without trying to alter that. He can be stuck in his ways at times and wants things a certain way but that was only because he was dedicated to his life plan.

He's worked extremely hard to manifest the future he's always dreamed of.

Anyone with common sense could tell by the sound of my clacking heels against the marble linoleum floors that I was nervous.

I really need this plan to work. I haven't figure out how I'm going to get us to a baby but one lie at a time would have to do for now.

I didn't pay thousands of dollars to have this body perfectly sculpted to ruin it by having kids. Not that that was ever an option but I can see why Kim Kardashian had surrogates. That's what I could use as a last resort.

When he sees how much I went through with the fertility I can hit him with the surrogate idea. That's it! Bre you're one smart cookie!

I watched Kaimen straighten his clothes in the side mirror of his car.

He was so sexy. His swag was unmatched.

I watched him make his way across street vibrating all that big meat energy. I bit down on my bottom lip thinking about the many rounds of make-up sex we had last night.

If I could get pregnant, I'm sure I'd be like that Ms. Whitley patient my husband tells me about. He said she was popping babies out like a busted bag of skittles. Lawed Jesus.

I'm trying to have just one baby and she done had a whole basketball team over there. Well, I ain't really trying.

"Glad you made it," I kissed him on the lips.

"You know I'm not missing this. I want to be at every appointment. I got you! I'm here for you through it all. Good or bad the highs or the lows. I'm riding with you woman," he assured me.

It was killing me what I was doing but he left me no choice.

"Thank you, baby. I'm scared but we got this."

"Yep, we got this," he lowered his head to kiss the top of my hand.

We made our way to Dr. Green's office. She had more patients waiting today so it looked even more legit than the last time.

Good job girl. She's turning out to be confirmation of money well spent.

"Hello," Dr. Green welcomed us into her office.

"Hello," we sang in unison.

"Well, I got your test back and we have some work to do. Bre we need to get your body healthy enough to house a baby. Right now, your body is viewing a baby as a foreign object so it's rejecting the conception. I can give you some injections for that. Once we're done with that treatment, we can start trying invitro fertilization. How does that sound?"

Kaimen locked eyes with me waiting for me to answer.

"It sounds amazing!"

"Well, let's get a baby in you then," she smiled.

"Baby, I have to get back to the office but I want you to fill me in on everything!"

Excitement beamed in his eyes as I kissed his lips before making his exit.

"I hate lying to him," Dr. Green confessed as worry tainted her eyes.

"Well, get out of your feelings about it! I can gladly send you back to the gutter I pulled your sinking career out of. You owe me and the way you're going to repay me is to help me keep my husband. If I don't give him a baby, he's going to leave me! I can't lose him. He's the love of my life Lydia!"

I looked down at my vibrating phone. It was Tamara. I was supposed to meet up with her after this appointment.

"I'm just trying to figure out what's next. What's going to happen when you don't get pregnant? Especially, when you know it's not possible."

"You let me worry about that. You just stay in your lane and play your role," I snatched my purse from the chair and walked out of her office.

She's worried about the wrong thing. As long as she keeps cashing them checks she can keep her bothered conscious to herself.

This body wasn't sculpted to perfection just to be ruined by birthing a child. I would do it if I could but I just can't.

I stormed past the receptionist I was paying. I allowed Lydia to take on a few more clients to make the office look legit.

Just in case Kaimen popped up I didn't want anything making him suspicious. I just need a little more time.

My mind was racing just as fast as my car as I shot over to the Southwest side to the Turkey Leg Hut.

The line was always ridiculously long but I knew the owners so I was considered V.I.P. The husband and wife duo were taking over the city with those turkey legs that had the meat falling off the bones. The drinks were potent and the vibe was unmatched.

I waived at Tamara who received hateful stares and eye rolls as she walked past those waiting to still get in. They watched us with envy in their eyes and I couldn't blame them.

"Hey girl!" Tamara leaned in and kissed me on the cheek.

"Hey boo. I was running a bit behind. Lydia had me held up whining about how she's uncomfortable lying to Kaimen. I don't pay her to have feelings. I pay her to do what I say!" I lifted my oversized glass of Hennessey Punch as I attempted to wash away Lydia's complaints.

"I can understand where she is coming from. I felt the same way back in the day when I dated you and found out you were lying to me."

"Not today Tamara. I can't deal with your crap too!"

My glass was bigger than my head so I couldn't slam it down on the table like I wanted.

I was getting sick and tired of people.

I was already on pins and needles because I know Allacia saw what was going down between Ario and I.

When I found out she knew Parelle, even though I don't know how, I lost it! I know he told her all my business but I'm just no sure of how much.

I was just waiting to see what she wanted because I know that trick wanted something.

"Listen, all I'm saying is consider telling your husband the truth," she reasoned with me.

"I want to Tamara but I just can't take the risk of losing him for good. I'm so in love with that man. He's changed me for the better and I never thought a man could do that for me."

"I know Bre but this lie could end very dangerously if he finds out. You're playing with his emotions and people don't take that well."

"I know. Every time I start to tell him I choke on the words. If he rejects me, I'm scared I'll go back to that dark place. You remember how bad it got with us back in the day. How needy and depressed I was. It took me a long time to love myself and feel that I deserved to be loved. I won't go back to being a nobody who's broken beyond repair."

"I get it. You know I got your back. I will always love you. I tried to show you that but you wanted something different the entire time we were together."

"I just was afraid to be myself Tamara. It wasn't about you. I've always kept you close because you're the only one that knows the real me. I need you. Always and forever."

"I know. You can appreciate me by paying for the tab I'm about to run up," she laughed breaking the tension.

******

Tamara and I were watching people start to feel their drinks and two-step in the center of the outside patio aisle.

They Zydeco music blared through the speakers washing away the torment going on in my mind concerning my marriage.

"Look what we have here."

The voice sent chill through me and the punch I had guzzled hit reverse and was on its way back up my throat.

Phillip Price. As long as I live, I will never forget his voice.

"What do you want Phillip?" I spat.

"Is that anyway to greet your old boss?"

"You weren't my boss you were my-"

"Go ahead and say it. Your pimp! I see you on all them fancy billboards and in those commercials. Niggas don't believe me when I say I use to pimp you," he gave a throaty laugh.

Embarrassment began to entwine itself around my heart making me feel as I would die from humiliation.

Tamara knew everything about me. She was with me through it all as I spiraled out of control. It was just something about hearing Phillip say those words that transported me back to the past.

"Leave me alone Phillip!" I whispered through clenched teeth trying not to make to make scene.

"Do your husband know about your past? He's that big-time baby doctor ain't he?"

"What do you want Phillip?!"

"Oh, you'll find out soon enough. Here take this," he slid me his card.

What does this negro need with a business card?

I looked down as if some type of incurable infectious disease would eat away my flesh if I touched it.

"Take the card or I can drop by her husband's office and express my concerns. I'm curious to know just how much he knows about his precious wife."

I snatched the card up and stuffed it in my purse.

"It was nice seeing you again...what are you going by these days again?"

"Brechelle," I answered dryly.

"Yeah, that's it," he laughed walking off.

"Are you okay?" Tamara asked.

"No, I have to get out of here," I pulled a wad of cash out and left it on the table.

I didn't wait for her to answer as I maneuvered though the crowd.

I was an emotional basket case as I sped back to work. I didn't want to go home and run the risk of my husband being there.

SSSKKKRRRRRRR!!!

The tears blinded me so I barely missed the oncoming truck. I accidently drifted in the other lane.

"You stupid-" I heard him yell out the window as I sped by struggling to gain control of the wheel.

I pulled into the parking lot of my practice, "No! No! No!" I screamed as panic consumed me.

The more I tried to bury who I once was the more it was manifesting to haunt me.

I pulled the visor down so I could see how horrible I looked. I reached into my purse and pulled out my foundation and eyeliner.

My makeup was waterproof but I just want to reapply it a smidge to make it pop. Just because I'm a mess doesn't mean I have to look like it.

"So, you just don't work anymore, huh?" Ario started with me as soon as I sat my purse down on my desk.

"I'm not in the mood Ario," I could feel sorrow closing my throat.

"What's wrong?"

I couldn't speak. Tears poured from my eyes. I felt trapped by my own life and situations I created from just trying to get what I know I deserved.

Ario rushed over to embrace me.

"You know you can talk to me about anything," he assured me lifting my chin.

He leaned in to kiss me.

"I can't believe you! You're still trying to take advantage of me even now! Get out of my office Ario! You ain't no different from the rest of these niggas."

"Why you trippin' like this is new for us?"

"I'm not on that anymore. I want my marriage and you know your sister caught us the day of your mama's funeral!"

"She ain't gone say nothing. She hates Kaimen."

"Exactly! She would tell him just to hurt him!"

"She wouldn't hurt me though. She's not going to say anything. Trust me."

"Nigga I don't trust you as far as I can see you."

"You know what. You clearly need some time alone. We have a consult in an hour so get your mind right. Here maybe this will help you," he tossed me the small glass container with the white powder inside.

Ario and I often used cocaine as an escape when we got under pressure. Between dealing with this family and our practice it was our only way out we felt at times to find some sense of peace.

"Whatever," I said.

"Yeah, aight. Just do what you need to do so we can make this money. I'll see you in an hour."

He locked the door before leaving out and I dropped in the chair like a ton of bricks.

I sprinkled the powder on the back of my hands and inhaled.

The high immediately pushed me back in my chair. I could feel my cares fading away.

This was just what I needed.

Chapter 13

ARIO

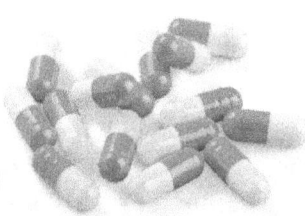

I watched as my surgery team positioned Phyllis on the table. Her long black hair was tucked under the mesh hair net. They stretched her arms out. First her left and then her right. The anesthesiologist was sitting above her head on a silver stool checking his measurements.

"Hey Dr. Yarbrough," Dr. Sloan greeted me.

She was assisting Bre and I on this surgery just in case we ran into something unexpected while Phyllis was on the table.

Dr. Sloan was plastered across medical magazine all over the world for her groundbreaking research.

I use to knock her back lose every now and again but she decided to get married on me. She ain't the cheating type so I settled for just being her friend.

"Dr. Sloan," I greeted her with a warm smile. "So, what's new with you?" I sparked conversation while we scrubbed in.

"Nothing much. This is weird and I hate to bring it up right before surgery," she stammered.

"What is it?" I stopped washing my hands to give her my full attention.

"I was on a surgery with her dad a couple of days ago. My condolences on the loss of your mother. I know this is a hard time for your family but-"

"For God sakes spit it out Eva," I demanded.

"Your dad doesn't seem like he's all there mentally. We were doing a simple liver transplant and he was struggling to get through a procedure he's done over a hundred times. I covered for him but people are starting to whisper and talk. You know how it is in hospitals."

"Thank you for letting me know. I'll investigate it some more. I really appreciate you for stepping in."

"No worries. This hospital is your family's legacy. I got your back. Besides, who else is going to give me crazy amounts of money for my farfetched research ideas," she laughed.

"Those ideas have brought a lot of money to our hospital. It was a no brainer to invest in you. Now let's assign some genitals," I said escorting her into the surgery room.

While I worked on Phyllis my mind was racing. It wasn't like Bre to miss a surgery, especially this one. She connected with Phyllis and was excited to perform this surgery on her.

"Felicity. Call Dr. Brechelle for me please," I instructed one of my surgery technicians.

"Sure thing," she said reaching for my phone.

Felicity has been working with me for years so nothing in or on my phone would shock her.

We all listened to the phone ring over and over until it went to Bre's voicemail.

As far as my father went now would be the perfect time for me to figure out how to get him removed from the board and me added in his spot.

Once that happens, I will work on having him declared incompetent so I can't get rid of Kaimen once and for all.

He sticks to dad like glue in hopes of slithering in like the snake he is. I refuse to leave my future in his bitter hands.

Kaimen could never cut it as a surgeon so he opted to be a gynecologist. He's such a perv I wouldn't be surprised if deep down inside he became that to play in vaginas all day.

He didn't have much experience before marrying Bre. She was literally the second woman he dated. Before his glow up he wasn't as appealing. My mother dragged him to every dermatologist in the United States trying to clear his face up.

Once it did it was like he snagged Bre before it broke out again.

I didn't even want Bre like that but I only messed with her to spite Kaimen.

I pushed my family from my mind so I could fully focus on Phyllis' surgery. When I was done, she would be flawless.

She was in for a painful recovery but I was hoping it would boost her esteem and help embrace her identity.

Whatever Bre was doing I hope it was worth it. She never misses a big surgery so I was a bit worried about her.

This surgery was the only thing on our schedule today so after this I was heading home.

I loved my sister but having Allacia crash at my house was starting to be an invasion of my privacy.

People believe because of the way I act that I have a parade of women galivanting through my home but I don't.

If I were to be transparent, I've wanted to settle down for quite some time but it's challenging finding your equal. Someone who speaks to your heart and soul while pulling the best out of you.

I want what my parents had. It wasn't perfect but it produced a legacy that was passed down to their children. It fostered growth, change and prolific accomplishments in both of their lives.

They both thrived as unit but maintained their identities as individuals. Their mutual love and respect for one another was everything.

If I don't have that then I don't want anything.

Until then I had to deal with my annoying sister. It was time Allacia grew up and start finding her way.

If she doesn't want to be a doctor then she needs to figure out how exactly she plans to leave her mark in this world.

******

We ran into some complications with Phyllis' surgery so what should've taken us about six hours max turned into a grueling twelve hour surgery.

By the time I left I was exhausted. I tossed my briefcase and my other belongings in the passenger seat of my Corvette.

I take the scenic route home so I could max out the speed on the dash. We lived on the outskirts of the city so I didn't have to worry about other cars often. It was my way of blowing off steam after work.

"Dang," I smash the steering wheel with my fist.

A cop was coming up behind me quick. I pulled to the side of the road. The last thing I needed was to become a hashtag. A black man ain't safe trying to make it out his front door and back these days. It doesn't matter who you are or what you do. They are killing us all the same.

"Mr. Yarbrough what did I tell you about speeding through my streets?" Officer Montoya scolded me.

He was an older white cop we favored Stone Cold Austin. He was cool and normally let me go.

"I'm just trying to get home. I just finished a twelve-hour surgery and I'm exhausted."

"I get it but I don't want to have to scrape you up off these streets Ario. You're doing amazing work over at that hospital. You know I owe you for the deal you gave me on my wife boob job," he laughed.

"How are you enjoying those," I joined him.

"She's four months pregnant let's just say that," he fist bumped me.

"Yes indeed, doc!"

"Listen, slow down and get home safe," he tapped the top of my car and walked back to his.

Officer Montoya was a cool dude. I did as he asked and dropped my speed.

I was only about ten minutes away.

I nodded at the security guard as I entered through our estate gates.

There was a car I didn't recognize in my driveway. It was almost midnight so Allacia having someone in my house this late was unacceptable. Her needing somewhere to crash versus her being laid up in my house was not going to work.

I'm starting to see why my dad is so hard on her. Allacia had no anchor in life and she was drifting in dangerous waters.

I dragged my body out the car and headed inside.

The house was pitch dark and eerily quiet.

"Alli?" I called out but she didn't respond.

I placed my briefcase on the floor and grabbed my pistol from the hidden holster under my kitchen cabinet.

Switching the safety off I headed towards Allacia's room.

I could hear whispering on the other side of her door.

"Didn't you hear me calling you?" I burst through her door.

"Don't be barging in here like you're my daddy or something Ario!"

The sketchy dude standing next to her was clearly on the wrong side of the tracks. His bald head and strong brow area gave his sunken eyes a hateful darkness.

I gripped my gun tighter as we stared each other down.

"You in my house and it's time for your company to leave."

She rolled her eyes at me but did as I asked.

"Phillip, let me walk you out."

The hoodlum made his way past me with an exaggerated pimp walk.

I was prepared for him to do anything. I was at the gun range three times a week sometimes more. When I shoot it was to kill.

I peered through the curtains in the living room while she continued to speak with him. I don't know what Allacia was up to but I know it was no good judging from this negro.

I was itching for her to come back in the house. What was she thinking bringing this negro in here?

"Don't start," Allacia rolled her eyes.

"That man can come back here and rob me blind! You got this nigga all through my house and you out of line for that. You are a guest here don't be having random niggas all through my house Alli!"

"I ain't no kid Ario!"

"Then stop acting like one! You need to get your crap together so you can stop bouncing from one house to the next."

"What you think I'm doing?"

"I know you better not be doing it with that nigga!"

"What does it matter to you?"

"You know if don't nobody got your back I do. Don't do that! I ain't going to tell you nothing wrong baby girl."

"Look, I'm not doing nothing illegal or nothing but I'm trying to get my business started. Phillip knows some people. We just got caught up talking about business and time got away from us. I would never disrespect you or your home."

"I believe you but don't be having sketchy niggas in my house Alli," I warned her.

"It won't happen again."

"Eva pulled me to the side at work today. She was telling me about an incident with dad that happened during surgery. She thinks his mental capacity is diminishing."

"Have you talked to him?"

"No. He's been dodging all of us since mom died. If I can prove he's incompetent I can have him removed from the board and take his place."

"What makes you think they'll give you the seat and not Kaimen?"

"A few of the board members approached me about a year ago with a proposition to take dad's position. I declined the offer but they assured me I could be voted in without any issues."

"Why can't you just tell them you want the spot now then?"

"Dad would fight me tooth and nail on it. If I can have him declared incompetent then I don't have to worry about it. I could then be over all his affairs not just on the board at the hospital. Then we can push Kaimen out of everything. Cut him off from daddy money once and for all."

"You cutting his wife off too?"

"Mind your business. Yea I am. I only mess with that girl to get to Kaimen. I've never actually slept with her she just gives me head."

"Gross and that's too much information."

"Well, get some rest big head," I kissed her on the forehead.

I hated Kaimen because Allacia did. Me and him had our problems since we were kids but not like him and Allacia.

I figured she would let me know when she was ready.

They used to be super close and then it was like she woke up one day and just started hating him.

I've always been protective over my baby sister. She was the only one I had in my life that believed in me and loved me despite me.

Anything I needed I know she would provide it for me. I would forever ride for that girl, even into the pits of hell if that's what was required.

I locked the house down and set the alarm. Despite what Allacia said I didn't trust that dude Phillip.

What kind of business could she have with him?

Chapter 14

KAIMEN

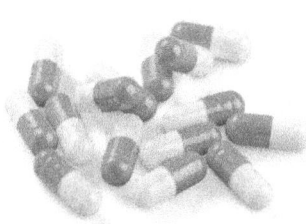

"Senovia can you take this over to my wife's office for me? I got another one of her files again," I handed her the folder.

Bre and I really needed separate works spaces.

"I...umm," she struggled to speak.

"What is it Senovia?"

"You know I'm the last one to speak on this but the last time I was there she was in the office with your brother. I walked in and she popped up from in front of him like she was you know."

"Why didn't you say something earlier?"

"I didn't think you would believe me. You know I don't care for Bre at all. I despise that woman and you deserve better."

"I understand and thank you. I'll run the file over myself then."

"Okay but make it quick your next appointment will be here in about thirty minutes. Please don't go over there starting trouble. I could be wrong it could've been perfectly innocent."

"I doubt it Senovia. My brother is a snake so it's not beneath him to try and seduce my wife. I won't go over there starting trouble though," I assured her.

Senovia was my baby. She kept me level and I was blessed to have her by my side. She always looked out for me and she would do anything to see me smile.

I've become fond of her over the years.

I decided to walk instead of drive over to the other building. I needed the extra time to cool off. If

Bre was messing with Ario I would make her life a living hell.

She could sneak around with anyone else but Ario was like spitting in my face while having the Corona Virus.

"Mr. Yarbrough, good to see you," Bre's front desk receptionist greeted me.

"I need to take something back to my wife," I kept walking.

"She's not here. She had an appointment but your brother is in."

"Oh, okay. I'll just leave it on her desk then."

"Sounds good. I'll let her know."

I pulled out my phone. I didn't see any appointments scheduled today for the fertility clinic. She wasn't with Ario because he's here.

What is Bre up to?

I know I've been putting a lot of pressure on her to have a baby. The last couple of days she's been aloof.

She's tossing and turning in her sleep. The recent night terrors cause her to wake up in cold sweats.

Something has been bothering her but every time I ask her about it, she just says it's work or something about our unborn child.

I want to believe her but it's just more to it. I know it. I can feel it in my gut.

"Surprised to see you here," Ario stopped me in the hallway leaving Bre's office.

"Yeah, I got one of Bre's files by accident so I dropped it off."

"Is she okay?"

"She's fine why do you ask?" I snapped.

"Look chill. I'm only asking because she's missing a lot of work lately. We had a major surgery yesterday and I couldn't get her on the phone. You know Bre don't miss no money and she love doing gender assignments."

"She's fine. Just stay away from my wife nigga."

"Stay away from your wife? You do realize we have a practice together, right? Women don't like insecure niggas lil' bro. It's not a good look on you."

"Insecure? Nigga you want everything I got! You keep clamoring for daddy's attention but you never get it because he hates everything about you. Why you think he use to beat you so much growing up?"

"Nigga I'll drop you where you stand," Ario slammed me into the wall.

The staff stopped what they were doing and watched us make a scene in the middle of the office.

"Get out of my office before I send you out in a body bag!"

I pushed him off me and straightened my clothes.

When I wanted to piss Ario off I would bring up how my dad would beat him just for the sun rising in the morning.

None of us knew why but it was like my dad had a special hate for Ario. My mother stepped in and stopped the abuse once she realized it was a direct assault on Ario.

My dad just saw in him what we all see now. He's an arrogant narcissist that needs to be taken down a peg or two.

I pulled out my phone once I was back in my car to call Bre but it went straight to voicemail. I left her a voicemail and then messaged her.

I don't know what she had going on but my gut was telling me she was up to something.

******

Esmeralda called and said dad wanted to have family dinner today. We haven't had a family gathering since mom's funeral. I can't really say I missed them either.

I still haven't heard from Brechelle all day other than the text message response that she will explain everything later tonight when she gets home.

When I arrived at my father's house Esmerelda had the staff still setting the table. I looked around and didn't see anyone even though Ario and Allacia's cars were parked out front.

I headed down the hall towards my dad's office. I peeked my head inside but he wasn't in there.

I kept walking down the long marble hallway. My parent's home looked more like a museum than a home.

I could hear low mumbles as I approached the library. The door was slightly ajar and I could hear Ario and Allacia in a deep conversation.

"I talked to the board. They're looking into dad's mental capacity. They'll be speaking with everyone that's been working closely with him on his surgeries. Eva said we can count on her to give a statement."

"Are you sure this won't backfire? They're bound to call Kaimen in at some point."

"Why would they? He's not on the board and he works in a totally different building. This has nothing to do with him or his practice."

"I guess you're right. You know better than I do."

"The plan is in motion we just have to wait for everything to play out."

I couldn't believe these ingrates! They were planning to get dad removed from the board so Ario can take over.

I've been hearing whispers that they've been trying to get Ario to replace dad for over a year now. I guess the rumors are true. I can't believe he didn't jump at the opportunity to replace him.

I guess he was only passing it up out of respect for mama.

When I made it back to the family room my dad was seated at the head of the table as usual.

"Hey daddy. How are you feeling today?"

"I'm doing as well as can be expected. How have you been son?"

Before I could answer Ario and Allacia appeared at the table to take their seats.

"Same ole' same. Just trying to keep my head on straight. Have you been watching your back at the hospital? I heard they trying to remove you from the board."

Allacia started to strangle on the sip of wine she took when she sat down.

Ario gave me a glare that could kill but I didn't care.

"I would like to see them try!" My dad spat.

"Something about your mental capacity since mom passed," I continued.

"You sure hearing a lot to be just now saying something," Ario chimed in.

"I wouldn't be surprised if you weren't the mastermind behind it all."

"It would only make sense wouldn't it? I've been busy bringing money into the hospital while you're off chasing around your wife. Where is Brechelle anyway?"

"What I tell you about asking about my wife nigga?"

My dad kept eating as if nothing was going on at all. He was completely unbothered by the foolery.

"Don't be like that Kaimen. Bre's family and I ain't seen her at work or around the estate lately. Everything okay with you two? You can't give her a baby maybe she out finding a nigga who can," he scoffed.

I took my dinner knife and tossed it in his direction.

"Nigga I'll kill you," Ario yelled pulling his pistol from his holster.

"Who brings a gun to dinner?" Allacia asked.

My father was still cutting away at his steak as if we weren't about to kill each other.

Was Ario right? Did dad check out on us?

"Nigga you ain't gone shoot nobody. Put that gun away."

"Mr. Yarbrough?"

"What?" We all yelled in unison.

"Mr. Cliff," Esmerelda clarified. "Mr. Winston is here to see you," she stepped to the side to allow the tall gentlemen in the room.

"You think we playing about our money Cliff?" He snapped.

"Watch how you talk to my dad!" Ario stood from the table brandishing his gun.

"Don't threaten me with a good time. If you pull you better not be afraid to use it. Last I checked you ain't dropped a single body so I doubt if you're going to pull that trigger. Me on the other hand. I have no qualms about pulling mine."

I had no idea where he was hiding that assault rifle but it would be effective enough at killing every one of us if he wanted to.

"I told you I was going to get your money. It's not like I can go to the bank and just pull out four million dollars," he cut away another piece of his steak.

Has this man lost his mind?

I was sitting there in a rage praying Ario would pull that trigger and drop this fool.

As usual he was all talk. Mr. Winston was right. Ario was not about that life.

"I thought you might say that. Here is the account number. I need you to call the bank and issue a wire transfer."

"A transfer that large would require me to go inside the bank and I'm having dinner with my family right now. When I'm done, we can go to the bank. Would you like to join us for dinner until then?"

Mr. Winston was clearly irritated but what choice did he have? If he killed my dad then he wouldn't get his money.

"Daddy, why did security let him on the property to begin with?" I asked.

"I own the company they work for," he replied smugly.

"Daddy, ain't no way we are allowing you to leave with this man and go to the bank. We all rolling out. As a matter of fact, let's end this dinner and get this taken care of now," Ario suggested.

"I'm finishing my steak first Ario," my dad responded calmly.

We all shared confusing glares among one another. Dad was clearly off his rocker and I'm starting to think Ario's idea to have him removed from the board may not be such a bad idea.

"Dad why do you owe this man four million dollars?" Allacia finally ripped the band-aid off and ask what we all wanted to know.

"Y'all bring in money but not state of the art facility money. I had to pull from other resources to get our hospital to the level in which I wanted it to operate at. I had to do what I had to do."

"What's the account number?" Ario asked Mr. Winston.

Dad just kept eating his steak as if he didn't have a care in the world.

Mr. Winston reached inside of his blazer pocket and pulled out a card. He slid it over to Ario and all our eyes followed the sliding card.

He looked down at Ario through laced fingers as he examined the card. Ario pulled out his phone and scrolled through his contacts. When he found the number he was looking for he pressed the phone icon next to it.

Me and Allacia's eyebrows were creased with worry.

"Hello Ian, I need a favor. I need you to transfer four million to an account for me."

Ario was quiet listening to what I'm sure was a list of reasons he couldn't do that over the phone for him.

"I understand but that's why I called you. This is an emergency and if you can make this happen I can be there within the next hour to sign the proper documents."

Ario was quiet again.

"That'll work as well. I'm at my father's home."

Ario disconnected the call.

"Mr. Winston, please verify your account. You'll find the funds have been pushed through."

We waited in silence as the man pulled out a separate device.

"It's been a pleasure doing business with you," he smirked.

"Now, please leave my father's home," Ario demanded.

Mr. Winston shrugged and did as he was asked.

How many faces was this negro fixing? He had enough to just have four million dollars moved just like that? I need to stop catching babies and start cutting faces.

"I'll get you back for that son," my dad assured him nonchalantly.

"Oh, you most definitely will dad. That's a nice amount of money. I've been saving since I graduated college."

"That's chump change to you," my dad scoffed.

"It's still my chump change dad. You know what? I'm going to let you have it tonight. I'm going home."

"I'm coming with you," Allacia jumped up from the table as if it was last call for alcohol before the club closed.

I just sat there in utter shock by what had transpired. My dad was just sitting there finishing dinner unphased.

He is clearly not in his right frame of mind. It's only a matter of time before he hurts himself or someone else.

Chapter 15

BRECHELLE

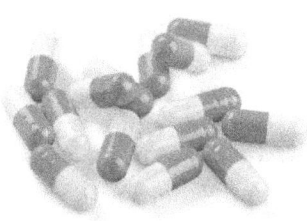

The way I was shaking you would think I'm not accustomed to being in sketchy allies. I'm not proud of my past but I've definitely outgrown it. My Mercedes was parked on the other side of the green rust-pitted dumpster that was leaking some type of unidentifiable liquid. I jumped at the sound of the rattling wheel of the homeless man's shopping cart.

KKSSHHH!

The sound of something glass hitting the cracked cement fell from the homeless man's cart.

"You're banned!"

The bouncer yelled as he flung the drunk man into the cart.

"Get off my stuff," the homeless man grumbled as he scurried to retrieve his things and put them back into his cart.

Both of their body orders were swirling through the vents of my car made my nose burn.

If Phillip wasn't here in the next five minutes I was burning off. I didn't have time to play these games with him.

The hundred thousand he was asking for was chump change. He didn't know it but I gave him a rundown about how Kaimen's family was keeping all the money. I told them those billboards and commercials weren't nothing but a ploy and I don't see a dime outside of my regular salary.

The jingle of keys caused my neck to snap in their direction.

He finally showed up.

I anchored my attention on his face and it was fixed. His eyes were stormy with destruction swirling in the midst.

"Open the door so I can get in."

I reluctantly did as he asked.

"Here. All of it is in there," I assured him.

WAP!

"What's wrong with you?!" I screamed. "This not like back in the day! You can't be putting your hands on me!"

His hands were wrapped around my throat so fast I didn't have time to react. I could feel my pulse starting to slow.

When he let me go, I started hysterically coughing so hard I thought I was going to dislodge a lung.

"A little birdie told me that you're a liar. This lil' birdie told me you are loaded just like your brother-in-law you practice with. This same birdie also said y'all messing around too. So, you are in fact just as I remember Brennon," he snarled.

"Don't you call me that! That's not my name anymore!"

"I'll call you whatever I want! Now get them clothes off!"

"What?"

"If you can huh you can hear! Don't make me ask again!"

"Look, I can get you what you want. Please just don't do this. Please!" I pleaded with everything in me.

Phillip was a foul piece of trash that no man or woman should ever have to be violated by. He hated himself and he spewed it on other people.

Inside I was praying that God would protect me and not allow this man to rip my soul from me again.

"You know what? I don't like this new you anyway. You ain't as cute as you think. I want two-hundred fifty thousand in a week. Just in case you think you gone go to the cops or something just know I still got these."

He held of his phone revealing sick pictures of me in compromising acts prior to my sex change.

The tears came harder and I was undone.

His mouth pulled to one side in a smug satisfaction before getting out of my car.

Phillip found me in a dark place. Tamara and I had just broken up because she was the first person I came out to. Like any woman she was hurt, angry and confused. I was blessed because her love was true. She eventually got over it without exposing me but once I told her I didn't care who knew.

My mother always had an idea and my dad was never around. My mother wasn't hateful but she was old school. I couldn't stay in her house and dress like a woman so I left.

I was homeless and that's when I met Phillip. At first, I thought he loved me and genuinely understood but nothing was further from the truth.

He almost killed me trying to get away but I did it. One of my regulars paid for my reassignment surgery. He also put me through medical school before dying. That's when I started back tricking. I was always grateful for what he did for me.

Remembering the kindness the old man showed me made me think of Kaimen. He was always a gentleman. He treated me like a queen from day one. It was time I tell him my tea.

I wanted to tell him once I realized we were getting serious but I was scared he would leave me. Each time I worked up the courage it quickly faded away.

At first, I didn't want to get rejected then it was all about not losing the first man I fell in love with.

Things between us were so unproblematic until he started nagging me about having a child. In the beginning I made that noticeably clear that I didn't want children.

We had just started dating and was doing the question thing where you learn about each other. I didn't care about losing him at that point so I expressed that children weren't an option for me.

It was like he knew I was hopelessly in love with him so he switched up on me with the baby thing.

I slowly started to resent him which is what led to me doing special favors on his brother. I didn't like Ario like that. He was just something to do when I was triggered by Kaimen.

Ario was cold and complex. He didn't care about anything but himself and his practice. He was as arrogant as they came but he was a brilliant plastic surgeon. He was often flown all over this country to do what other swore couldn't be done.

He was nothing like my baby which is why I need to come clean. I can't have Phillip hanging this over my head. I had to take the power from him.

When I made it to the house, I didn't see my husband's car so I figured he was working late. I decided to head to his office because I had to tell him this while I had the nerve.

If I waited too long I would never tell him what he deserves to know.

The office was closed when I arrived but his car and his nurse car were both parked outside.

Senovia has been Kaimen's nurse since he opened his practice. She basically ran his practice for him. I guess she never mentioned to him what she walked in on because Kaimen never questioned me about it.

Not once have I had problems with her other than how close she was with my husband. It wasn't uncommon in the medical field. Your nurses could make or break your practice so I understood to a certain degree.

I used my key to let myself in. The lights were off apart from the screensaver with the practice logo and helpful tips for new mothers.

The diffuser steam smelled of lavender and vanilla. It was my idea to add it to calm the mothers and babies.

"Are you kidding me?" I yelled when I found Kaimen's lips locked with Senovia.

Smack!

"Brechelle go home. I'll be there soon," he brushed off my slap with a dismissive wave of his hand while she watched with a smug grin on her face.

I did as he asked not to comply but because if I stayed, I would lose my license and I worked too hard for it! I'm not jeopardizing that for him or anyone else.

Since we are cheating tonight, I guess I'll go find comfort in the arms of his brother. This time I'm going all the way with him.

Chapter 16

ARIO

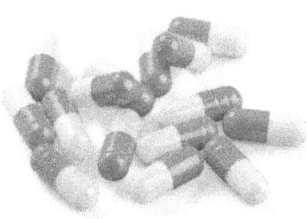

BAM!

BAM!

BAM!

I put my glass of scotch on the table and grabbed my pistol. After Allacia had that sketchy dude over here I wasn't sure if I would eventually be robbed. Mr. Frank old self at the security gate just be letting anybody up in here.

I'm still waiting for my dad to pay me back but paying the gambling debt was the perfect ammunition I needed to take his spot on the board. Once I proved to them he was involved in illegal acts his spot was as good as mine. I would be able to have the hospital pay me back the money.

"Girl, what are you doing at my house this late? I don't have time for your husband crap tonight. I had a long day."

"I want to have sex with you."

"Girl that sound so dry," I laughed and walked off.

"I'm serious!"

"No, you mad at my brother. What he do now?"

"I caught him and Senovia kissing."

"Oh yeah they been messing around just as long as y'all been married," my shoulder gave a slight shrug.

"Why didn't you say anything?"

"That ain't my business."

"Look, I didn't come here to talk. Come on and knock my back loose. I've made you wait long enough."

"You ain't make me wait on nothing. One thing I ain't never pressed over and that's some cat."

"We doing this or not?"

"I ain't gone turn down nothing but my collar," I said scooping her up in my arms.

I gently laid her on the couch. It was revenge sex but I didn't care.

She looked nervous but I wasn't sure why. We've been fooling around for a few years now. We've never gone all the way and I wasn't tripping about it. I had plenty of women to do that.

"What the-"

"What's wrong?" She straightened her back.

"Did you think I wouldn't be able to tell? You had gender reassignment! You know we do this for a living! Your vaginal canal is shallow Bre! You foul!" I yelled fumbling to stuff my junk back in my sweatpants.

"I...I"

"I knew it was something about your bougie tale," Allacia folded her arms defiantly.

"Oh my God, "she slapped a hand over her mouth.

Bre grabbed her stuff so fast and bolted out the door.

"That's what you get," Allacia scolded me before returning to her room.

This whole time I had no idea Bre was transgender. Why would she take away my choice like that? Why would she take away my brother's choice?

I filled the rim of my glass to the top. What Bre did was really jacking up my psyche. Not just that she toyed with my sexuality!

"Did you know she was transgender Allacia?"

"You think I would've let you keep messing around with Bre or whatever her name is if I knew that? C'mon bro give me some credit. The question is does Kaimen know?"

"You know he ain't have much experience before Bre.

"But that's what he does for a living. Look at coochie's all day. How could he not?"

"He ain't never snagged nobody that looked like Bre. To be honest he probably ignored all the signs. If he knew there's no way he would have her trying to get fertility treatment."

"I guess but you never know with that snake."

"I know why I don't like the nigga Alli but why did you and Kaimen fall out?"

"Just leave it alone Ario. My secrets have caused enough damage and I just don't want to get into it."

"Secret? What secret involves Kaimen?"

"ARIO LEAVE IT ALONE!"

My gut wanted me to dig deeper but the pain in her eyes kept my need for answers at bay.

"Okay baby sis. I'll let you have it for now. Get some sleep, big bro loves you. If that nigga hurt you best believe I'm gone kill him."

"You worry to much. I love you too," she hugged me so tight it made goosebumps form on my arms.

This family's secrets are spilling over and it appears we don't know each other like we think.

Chapter 17

ARIO

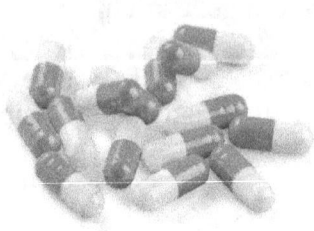

"Don't you have to be at work?"

"Don't you need a job?" I snapped back at Allacia.

It was too early for her smart mouth.

"I'm taking the day off. Mind your business."

"Are you okay bro? I know that was some wild mess that unfolded last night. I couldn't stop wondering if Kaimen knows."

"What, you gone tell him or something?"

"I agree with him never being a lady's man. We both know he didn't really glow up until after medical school so wasn't no girls giving him no cutty," she joked. "He did marry Bre shortly after. I don't think he had enough experience to observe what you did last night. That's my final answer."

"I don't want to talk about that Allacia. I was messing around with Bre and the whole time she was once a man. That's screwing with my mind on the real. Like I feel some type of way for real sis. You don't do that to nobody. She took away my choice time after time."

"Well, it's not all on Bre you chose to mess with your brother wife and I guess Karma just came back a different way."

"Karma? Tuh"

"Well, I got some errands to run. If you need me just hit my phone," she kissed me on the cheek.

A storm was brewing inside me that only made me drink more. I didn't bother eating I just kept drinking. One after another I tossed them back until I started to feel numb.

With Allacia gone the walls started to speak louder and louder.

I went into my bedroom and pulled the shoebox from under the bed. I took out the gold box that housed the white power that always made me feel better.

I locked my bedroom door and pulled my nightstand in front of me.

After making sure it was thoroughly broken down, I made three neat lines.

I pulled the hundred-dollar bill from wallet and rolled it up. I inhaled all three lines back to back.

"I need to go tell Kaimen who his wife really is," I reasoned with myself. "Yep, gone head and crush his soul Ario," I continued.

My conversation with myself made perfect sense. I grabbed my keys off the hooks and hopped in my car.

I watched the speedometer rise as I pressed my foot against the petal. Eighty. Ninety. One Hundred. One-Twenty.

BOOM!

I knew I was in trouble once my tire blew.

All I could hear in the back of my mind is Officer Montoya scolding me for speeding down his road.

Every muscle in my body went rigid. I drew in a long breath trying to brace myself as much as possible for the impact.

AAARRRGGHHH!

Everything in my body hurt forcing me to bellow out in pain. The next thing I knew everything went black. I prayed I would see my mama when I crossed over because I just know I'm dead.

******

I groaned in pain but I felt like my ears were superglued shut. Was I dead but still somehow able to feel?
"Help! Help!" I panicked.

I tried to jerk my body but couldn't move. I finally forced my eyelids open and was heartbroken to still be on this God forsaken earth.

Mama why didn't you come for me?

To my dismay I only saw Dr. Sloan.

"Easy now," she rested her hand on my chest. "Ario. Can you hear me?"

"Yeah, what happened.?"

"You went off into a ravine and totaled your sports car. They said you were intoxicated and speeding."

"I just had a couple of drinks."

"Your blood alcohol level was way past the drinking limit Ario. I had to view your tox screen before I operated on you. You had cocaine in your system as well," she whispered. "I fixed that so it won't show up anywhere but what were you thinking?"

"Operated on me?"

"Ario...you crushed both of your hands," she sobbed.

Her words started to make the world move in slow motion. I felt like I had stepped into a dream world; a horrific, nightmarish dream world.

Who am I without my hands?

"What did you do?" I hysterically panted lifting both of my hands in front of me. "How could you butcher me like this? What have you done?"

I cried like a newborn baby being pulled from his mother while breastfeeding.

I woke up alone with no hands. No one to comfort me or assure me everything would be alright.

If my mama were here, she would be cradling my head in her arms praying for my healing and mind. *I can't do this alone mama.*

"Ario, I'm here. I got you!" Allacia kissed my forehead.

"Mr. Yarbrough we're going to get you into rehab as soon as your able. Dr. Sloan did an amazing job. She very well may have saved your hands but we won't know for sure until the swelling has subsided. I'm confident she did what she's been known to do," the physical therapist assured me.

"Son you had a lacerated liver and a ton of other internal damage. They tried to discourage me because you're my son but they know I would've done everything in my power to rain down my wrath on them if they tried to keep me from operating on you. I know I've not been myself since your mother left us but seeing you on that table did something to me son. I know I've been hard on you but it's only because you are so much like me son. I'll be here every step of the way. You will operate again, I promise!"

My dad's warm tears weighted my heart. So many years I've longed for him to love me and see me. I've wanted him to let me know how he feels about me. I was no golden child but I was his child. I was grateful that he showed up in this moment because my hands were linked to my identity. I don't know who I am without them.

I didn't have my mom but my dad was trying to be here for me and I was grateful.

Tears poured from my eyes. Life as I knew it was over and it was all Bre's fault.

"Kaimen was in here earlier but he didn't think it would be a good idea if he were here when you woke up. He was really worried about you Ario," Allacia informed me.

That was a lot coming from her because she hated him. I guess he really was worried.

I couldn't think about any of this right now. The only I could do was stare at my bandaged hands with all the pins protruding from them.

What was I supposed to do now?

Chapter 18

KAIMEN

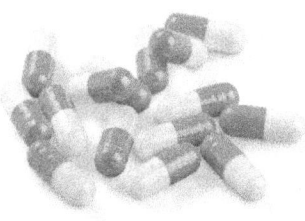

"So, did she pay the money?" I asked Phillip.

"Yep. I did as you asked and made her pay more. She was trippin' especially when I showed her them pictures."

"You gave me the only copy, right?"

"Yeah, I told you. I ain't tryin' to cross you man. This can be beneficial for both of us. You may need some muscle down the road."

"Oh, I'm not worried about that."

"Man, what the-"

I injected the syringe in his neck. His head made a thud when it hit the glass window.

The corners of my mouth turned up. I had no use of him anymore. The infertility clinic that Bre took me to was sketchy so I did some digging.

I mean I had to do some major digging to find out the dude's name behind the company.

The pictures that came up at first, I thought was Bre's brother.

I called in a couple of favors when I ran into some sealed court records due to the defendant being a minor.

When my connect pulled the cases Phillip's name was listed as the person that bonded the guy listed on the building out of jail a couple of times.

He wasn't easy to find but when I did find him, I was mortified by what he had to say. My heart stopped when he showed me the pictures.

Bre was transgender.

Bre had me feeling like a fool. Dragging me around to fertility clinics knowing there wasn't a uterus to carry a child.

Thoughts of how I would make Bre pay for what she did flooded my mind until I pulled into the driveway.

"Daddy! Daddy! Daddy!" Kaimen Jr. ran out to greet me.

Senovia stood in the doorway admiring our interaction. I should've married her instead of Brechelle but Senovia wasn't as flashy and accomplished as Bre. She was solid, loving, nurturing and she was the mother of my two children but just not enough of what I needed.

Bre worked so much it wasn't hard having an entire family on the side. Senovia was very understanding. She knew what she was getting into once our feelings started to change for one another.

"Dinner is already on the table, baby," Senovia kissed my cheek as I walked inside.

The smell of lasagna made my mouth water. I loved when she made dinner from scratch. It reminded me of when my mother would cook for us.

She would've hit the roof if she found out about who Bre really was.

Ario! I wonder if he knew? I doubt it. If he was messing around with Bre I can't wait to expose this to him and the rest of the family.

When I found out how Bre lied I was hell bent on returning the pain that was willingly spewed on me.

I would deal with all of that soon enough but for right now I just wanted to spend time with my family.

Something I deeply desired but could never have with Brechelle.

She'll pay for these lies.

Chapter 19

ALLACIA

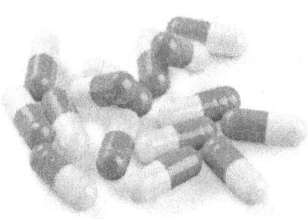

"What in the-," my words clogged my throat restricting my speech.

The hairs on the back of my neck stood at attention. I knew Kaimen was a snake but I didn't know he was a killer!

After Kaimen expressed his concern about Ario I felt it only fair I tell him about Brechelle. It was time our family started to heal and I was taking the first step.

When I was pulling into the estate he was going out but he was looking one way. He was talking to someone on his phone.

I hit a U Turn trying to catch up with him but he was driving with purpose. It was already late so I figured he was on call and I would catch up to him at the hospital until we ended up here.

I didn't have time to stop and check on Phillip or I would lose Kaimen.

I was insulted that Ario believed I would spread my legs for Phillip.

I sped past his dead body loitered to the side of the alley like the trash he was. I was careful to keep my distance from him.

Where is he going? This is not the way to my father's estate.

"Well snatch off my wig and call me bald," I laughed clapping my hands when I saw the little boy run out and hug my brother.

Senovia was standing in the door admiring him like he was father of the year or some crap. I knew they were a little too close for something.

She was way to attentive to him for them not be messing around. Bre would be able to see if had she not been running behind Ario.

I blame her for what happened to him. He started drinking non-stop when he found out who she really was. It messed with his mind and manhood.

I had every intention on ripping her life apart at the very seams.

I pulled out my phone to call my sister-in-law. I let the phone ring until she answered.

"Hey, you know where your husband's nurse Senovia lives?"

"Yeah, we've had dinner there before with her and them bad kids," she replied. "Why wassup?"

She sure was letting her ghettoness show.

"Well, I was visiting someone on the same street and saw Kaimen kissing her and those kids. It's weird but have you noticed how much her son looks like my brother?" I added gasoline to the fire without hesitation.

"Those kids don't look like my husband but is he still there?"

"Yep, I can see them eating dinner through the front window."

"Aight bet," she ended the call abruptly.

I thought about running to the gas station to get some snacks but I was afraid I would miss all the action.

I was right because it was only fifteen minutes before Bre pulled up barely putting the car in park before she jumped out.

BAM!

BAM!

BAM!

The look of surprise on Kaimen's face as she beat down the door was nothing in comparison to his expression to find his wife at the door.

"What are you doing here?" He asked her.

"I should be asking you that! Why aren't you at home with me? You told me you put an end to this when I caught y'all at the office!" She pointed her finger in his face.

"Get your finger out of his face," Senovia slapped her hand. "You won't disrespect him in front of me or our children!"

"Your...your...children," she gripped the door to maintain her balance because Kaimen just watched her crumble.

"Yes, my children. How long did you think I was going to keep begging you to make me a father Bre?"

"So you go off and make them outside of our marriage? How could you do this to me?"

"I felt bad at first but once I found out what you really were it paled in comparison to the lie you told me. Senovia, please take our children upstairs."

I was praying they didn't close the door or I would be out of range from hearing all this tea spill.

So he did know about Bre! I wonder how long has he known?

"What lie are you talking about Kaimen?" She asked him.

"Girl you know what lie he talking about," I whispered.

"Were you born male or female?"

"Kaimen don't do this. Please," I could see her chin quivering as she pleaded with him.

I didn't care for Bre but she didn't deserve this. They both appear to have just been running around doing them and lying to each other about it.

They lived in the same house day in and day out but had no idea what the other was doing.

Apparently, they had no idea who the other one really was either.

"You already did it Bre!" He tilted his head to the side.

She just stood there helpless.

"Answer my question," he continued to badger her. "Were you born male or female?"

"Male," she was barely audible from where I was parked.

"Get out of here and be out of my house before I get home in the morning."

"In the morning?"

"What did you think would happen once I found out? You've been dragging me around town like you can have kids and you knew the entire time you couldn't! I'm glad Senovia has my children. If you try to get anything in the divorce, I was ruin you! I will end what career you have left! Get out of here before I beat you down like the man you are!"

"ARRRGGGHH!

Brechelle let out a screeching that gave insight to the agony she felt when her hand got caught in the door.

Kaimen opened the door long enough only for her to pull her hand free.

Once he was back inside, I ran to her aid.

If he saw me it would've only made matters worse and I kept my thirty-eight in my purse. I wasn't afraid to let it off either.

She smelled of liquor and anguish. At first, I wanted to hurt Bre because I felt she didn't deserve to be in our family but she's earned her place here.

She's dealt with the same crap we dish out to each other daily. I hated that she didn't reveal her truth but it's her truth.

"C'mon let me get you out of here."

"Get off of me!" She pushed me. "This is exactly what you wanted! I'm not stupid! I know you hate me!"

"I've always thought you were shady but I've never hated you. I don't think."

"Whatever," she sobbed.

Bre has always been so confident and flawless. I don't think I've ever seen her this vulnerable.

"Trust me. You dodged a bullet with my brother. He's not what he appears to be either Bre."

"What do you mean?"

I stood there debating if I should share my dark secret with her.

"Kaimen raped me when we were teenagers. When I told my dad all he did was cover it up. My mother never knew either. That's why I hate him so much Bre. I'm sorry you just got caught in the cross-fire."

"What do you mean caught in the cross-fire?"

"I'm the one that let Phillip know who you are now. I'm the reason he found you," I confessed. "Once Parelle linked us up I was livid when I found out how you lied to us."

"You what?" She gasped. "How can you be so vindictive? That man was ready to kill not only me but your entire family. He would've just kept coming and coming for more money until someone killed him!"

"Someone did," I mumbled.

"What did you say?"

"Kaimen killed him. Right before he got here, he pushed him out of his car in this dark alley not too far from here," I explained.

The expression on Bre's face served a duality of satisfaction. First, for Phillip being dead. Second, she now has something she can hold over Kaimen's head so she wouldn't lose everything in the divorce.

"You may have just redeemed yourself."

I helped her from the ground while she held her other hand in place.

"You need me to drive you home?"

"Nah, I'm good. You better get out of here before he sees you. I'm sorry he hurt you Allacia."

Brechelle's eyes were pleading for me to feel her sincerity.

"Yeah, me too."

I helped Bre in the car and hit a quick jog to get back in mine.

She sped off without even making sure I was in my car safe.

"I should've known your messy self was behind Bre coming over here acting a fool."

I had no idea where Kaimen came from but all I knew was that I didn't want to be out here alone with him.

I fumbled to put my keys in the ignition so I could drive off.

"You still ain't learned about sticking your nose where it doesn't belong, huh?"

I could hear him screaming behind me as I burnt off.

I couldn't wait to tell Ario about everything that went down.

Chapter 20

ARIO

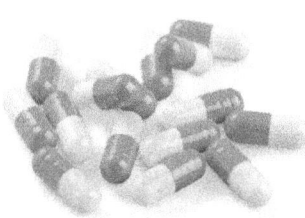

I looked at the squares on the ceiling. They had me in the VIP suite of the hospital but I was ready to go. They say doctors are the worst patients and now I see why. The unsuspecting patient may not know exactly what you should be doing but another doctor does. Most of the times we're better than the person taking care of us.

We know those who are incompetent. Those who snort and drink before they cut open a body or attempt to save a life.

I wanted them to try me so I could have all their licenses. I was already bitter about my life changing overnight. I wanted to blame Bre but I made the choice to drink and drive.

My healing process has been painful and slow. Tears flooded my eyes as I watched the nurse change the bandages on my hands.

Dr. Sloan did what she could but the scarring was deplorable.

"Dr. Yarbrough I know you're going to bounce back from this," the attending nurse encouraged me.

"From your lips to God's ears," I sighed.

She gripped my hands one final time as she gathered up the old bandages for disposal.

"How you feeling big bro?" Allacia barged through the door bumping rudely into my nurse.

I didn't have the energy for her shenanigans today.

"What you want Alli?"

"Don't sound so unenthusiastic," she scoffed.

"I got both my hands wrapped up and I don't even know if I can come back from this. Excuse me for not putting on the show that you deserve."

I watched Allacia's demeanor change.

"I'm sorry bro. I don't mean no harm. You got me so spoiled sometimes I get a bit selfish. I hope you know you're my world," she curled up in the bed with me.

"You're mine baby sis. What you run up in here with all that energy about anyway," I laughed.

Her messy but would just bubble over when it came to some drama.

"Did you know your brother has two whole kids by his nurse Senovia?"

"Oh, yea. She been popping kids out for that nigga. She two months pregnant now. Bre was a possession. She looked good on paper and in magazines but Senovia got his heart. She let Bre take the lead role and get all that money because it's just setting her kids up in the long run. They always treated me like the black sheep but I'm the one that know everybody dirt."

"You love making it seem like you the Don of the family or something," she laughed hysterically.

I loved seeing my baby sister laugh. She stopped really laughing a lot when we were kids. Talking about girls mature faster than boys and all this other crap. It was like one day she wasn't my innocent baby sister no more.

When she laughed it reminded me of a time when things were simpler.

Allacia jumped up out the bed to close the door all the way.

She eerily curled back up in the bed with me and she pressed her lips near my ear.

"Kaimen killed that dude I had at your house."

"What?"

"Shhhhh!" She slapped her hand over my mouth. "I saw him throw the body from his car and drive off. Dude in an alley not too far from his baby mama house."

I pressed the red nurse button on my oversized remote control.

"Yes, Dr. Yarbrough?"

"What are you doing?" Allacia snapped.

"I need my morphine."

Allacia flopped back on the pillow with the back of her hand against her forehead.

"Man, this too much! I need a hit," I joked trying to lighten the mood.

"I knew he was a lot of things Ario but I didn't know Kaimen was a killer."

"What? I don't put nothing past a nigga that crawl around in the dark scheming. Why would he kill dude though?"

"I was paying him to blackmail Bre. Kaimen was already looking into Bre's background and he hit her will everything when she popped up. I was sitting in the car when it all hit the fan. He protected that baby mama and his kids from that foolishness. Senovia was looking like she's been waiting for her time to shine. She was Omarion's level of unbothered the entire time it all unfolded."

I just shook my head. I didn't want to hear none of that but I know she was just trying to make sure I stayed up on what was going on in our family.

I can't believe I actually wanted to run this hospital but after all this mess I just want to go to Paris.

Dr. Sloan knows someone who is doing some cutting-edge research regarding stem cell regeneration. I may be able to get my hands back. That's all I care about right now.

I can't believe I cared about any of this at one point. Nothing like almost dying to put everything in perspective for you.

"Allacia, I know you're just trying to keep me in the loop but I don't care about any of that. The only thing I want is to hopefully get released in a few days so I can book a flight to Paris."

"Paris?"

"Yeah, there's a specialist there who may be able to help my hands snap back."

"They may do that on their own. You just had the accident. At least wait to see what your body does on its own."

"I know you don't want to be here alone so why don't you just come to Paris with me. We ain't built like them anyways. Let's just go."

"I can't leave daddy."

"That man don't care nothing about you."

"That's not true Ario. He's still my daddy."

"That man ain't been much of nothing since mama died. The only one he cared to be a father to is his murdering son. I'm done with the competition. I'm dropping this stupid vendetta."

"I can understand. No lie when I saw Bre breakdown after everything went down, I felt bad. He slammed her hands in the door and everything. I told her I was the one who contacted Phillip."

"How did that go?"

"She was heated. She burnt off on me leaving me to dodge Kaimen on my own. He came out of nowhere when I was getting into my car. You know I don't like being around him," she cut her eyes at me.

The two of them have both always had weird energy. The last time I pressed her for answers about it she shut me down. I have a gut feeling this is more than sibling rivalry.

"Here you are Dr. Yarbrough," the nurse extended her hand with the small paper cup.

I threw back the pills and carefully sipped the water the nurse held for me.

"These pills going to be kickin' in soon so you can stay or you can leave baby sister."

"You can get some rest. I'm going back to your house."

"You been feeding my fish?"

"Yes, I've been feeding those high maintenance fish."

"Not one better be dead either Allacia," I fussed as she waved me off closing the door behind her.

******

"What the-"

"I didn't mean to wake you son," my father's raspy voice was a surprise to hear this time of night.

I fumbled around trying to press the button on my phone to see the time but the wraps I wore like mittens made it impossible.

"It's three in the morning," my dad answered the question banging around in my head.

"Daddy, what are you doing up and out this time of morning?"

"I don't sleep since your mama left me. Her side of the bed is ice cold and her feet are no longer there to warm mine. I know you're trying to get me off the board. I don't blame you. I haven't been myself lately. Surgery was the only thing that felt normal in my life still. It's the one thing I had almost as long as your mother. The money has been transferred back into your account. I figured you could use it for your rehab."

"I don't even know if rehab will help me," I raised both arms in the air.

I didn't feel triumphant like Rocky though. I felt like Apollo Creed when he got the brakes beat off him.

"Just give it time. The body is a miracle in itself. After all these years we're still learning more and more every day. Do you know who you are without plastic surgery?"

"Pops, I don't know who I am with plastic surgery. If it wasn't for the drugs, I probably wouldn't admit that out loud."

"I know you think I was hard on you because I disliked you but that wasn't the case. You had so much of me in you that I tried to beat the bad parts out. I didn't know any better. I was only doing what my dad did to me. When I finally sat back I realized that you had more of my good than anything. The brilliance I exhibit when operating on kidneys you do the same with plastic surgery. You've been published so many times you've stopped counting I bet."

"That's long gone now," I whimpered.

I could feel the warm tears trail down my cheeks. The right tear stopped at the corners of my mouth while the tear from my left eye hit my bandage.

They were unwrapping them tomorrow before I leave. I was terrified to see my hands.

"It's okay to feel this but don't get stuck here. Don't give up. Out of all my children you're the most driven, relentless, stable one."

"Stable," I snickered.

"Yes. Stable. You have your moments but you're going to take care of business no matter what. I see y'all clearer than you realize."

"Is that why you're so hard on Allacia?"

"I did that girl a great disservice spoiling her the way I did. I'm trying to get put my foot down now."

"I think it's a little too late for that," I groggily pulled myself up on my pillow.

My dad shifted in the sunken worn visitor chair next to my bed. He lowered one leg and crossed the other leg over it.

Sitting here talking to my dad was weird. Like he said I thought this man hated my guts the way he use to beat me.

"I just don't want to die and she can't take care of herself. If you go to Paris she will be alone. I can't leave her with Kaimen," his eyes trailed away and plummeted into a dark place.

"Stop talking like that. Your stubborn self ain't going nowhere."

"We all have a number and when it's up, it's up."

"I'm proof that if it's not, it's not."

"True. Well, get some rest son. I know you want to rest but I'm having them bring you to the house for dinner before you get settled in."

"How did you know about Paris?"

"It's my job to know about everything. I'm not as senile as y'all believe I am," he smiled.

My dad placed his hat on his head. He looked back lovingly at me and nodded.

When the door closed behind my dad the tears wouldn't stop. My hands had a long way to go but my heart was on its way thanks to my dad.

I can't believe that we were plotting on him when the whole time he's just missing my mama.

He's trying to learn how to live and be a father to us without her.

When I look at my dad all I see is regret. I don't want that look in my eyes when I get old.

Chapter 21

CLIFF

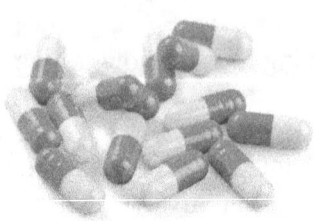

"Did you get everything I put on the menu?" I asked Esmerelda.

"Yes Sir. I made all of their favorites just as you requested."

I was proud of myself. I was finally starting to feel like the old me again. I stood admiring the table.

Everything was immaculate just like my wife use to do it.

I know she's so proud of me right now.

"AAARRRGGGGHHH!"

I could hear Bre yelling but I couldn't see her.

"Daddy, where you at?"

I barely recognized his voice. I've never heard Kaimen really raise his voice in this manner.

"Get your hands off that woman!"

"Nah, this ain't no woman."

"What are you talking about son?"

"Bre, tell my daddy what you are?"

"I'm not going to tell you again to keep your hands off her. I don't care what y'all got going on. You're not about to do this here!"

"Or what daddy?"

I have been out the streets for a long time now but I know a forty-four when I see one. He had it aimed in my face while Bre squirmed on the floor.

"You came in here to shoot me?"

"No, I came to expose all the secrets this family has."

"What's going on?" Allacia asked.

Her words faded away but fear was twisted in her face. Her eyes grew as big as saucers.

Ario was unfazed. He limped past Kaimen and sat at the dinner table.

"Oh, big bad Ario ain't scared of nothing, huh?"

"Nah, I'm just in pain. What is this about?"

"Well, you should know," his nostrils flared as he waved the gun around.

Kaimen looked like a mad man. He wasn't the poised, respectful, timid man he usually was when we were all together.

"Go sit down," he shoved Bre across the floor.

Allacia ran to her aid.

"Oh, now you want to help her? You were digging into her past just like I was. I mean his. Let's not mince pronouns," he spat.

Bre was clearly terrified of him.

"Son. What do you hope to achieve here today?" I asked him.

"I told you daddy. This is a reckoning for this family."

"You have some nerve! This family is the way it is because Dad hid how you raped me growing up! It was our dirty little secret. It's the reason he spoiled me. He wasn't doing that because I was his baby girl. He was spoiling me out of guilt."

"You what?" Ario interjected standing from table.

"Try me and I'll blow those precious hands off of your body," Kaimen threatened.

I cringed when Allacia spoke her truth. I wish I could've done the same thing when my wife was alive. I was scared this would kill her.

"Dad knew the whole time Ario," Allacia's eyebrows were knitted together in anger.

"What? Nigga I'm gone kill you!"

"She ain't even our real sister. She adopted fool!" Kaimen spewed more venom.

"That's enough!" I stood from table.

"Daddy is this true?"

I stood shoving the chair back quickly to run to her aid.

"Enough of the lies daddy! I'm adopted?"

"Yes," I finally admitted.

She dropped in the chair like a rug was being pulled from under her.

"I don't care if she's adopted. Why didn't you have him locked up for violating her? Then on top of that you punish her for how she dealt with it all these years. How are you going to try and push her into adulthood but you paralyzed her with childhood trauma long ago?"

"I...I.."

I tried to explain to my kids how I thought I was doing what was in all their best interest. I wish my wife were here. I don't know how to talk to these kids.

"You got a gun on all of us because you found out your wife use to be a man? You starting all of this because your lil' feelings hurt. I'm shocked because you got a whole family across town with that nurse from your job," Allacia blurted out.

"Family?" I was really confused now.

"Yes daddy, he got two grandkids you ain't never met across town," Allacia continued.

"I know what I did was wrong but you can't deny the love I have for you," Bre contended for her space in the conversation.

"You love me so much you were messing with my brother behind my back. You think I didn't know? The icing on the cake was that fake clinic you had me going to like you could have a child. You used your birthname which is how I found Phillip Price, may he rest in hell. Lie after lie you weaved together forming something that was never real. I'm glad I made children with Senovia. I hate you Bre!"

"I would be anything. Say anything. Go anywhere just to keep your love. Now that I know who you really are, I'm disgusted. You ain't no better than anyone else in this room. What you got us all held hostage here for? What you did to Allacia was unforgiveable. You're the monster here, not anyone else!"

WAP!

Kaimen brought the butt of the gun down across Bre's head.

Enough was enough.

Ario and I both lunged at him.

"Let go of the gun," I grunted trying to make sure the gun didn't go off.

Ario was having a hard time with his hands but he put his weight and elbows to use.

POP!

POP!

We all froze in time. I wasn't sure who got shot but I know one of us did. Ario's jaw dropped and snapped shut again.

"Son?"

"It's not me dad."

Our shared glares fell to Kaimen. Blood was now pouring from the side of his mouth and soaking through his shirt.

"Hold on Kaimen," I yelled applying pressure to the bullet wounds.

"Police! Freeze!"

Esmerelda or one of the other staff must've called them once they realized what was going on.

"I'm Dr. Yarbrough this is my son. He's been shot! I'm applying pressure to the wounds but get the paramedics here now!"

The cop kicked the gun away from us but never took his gun out of our faces. I could hear my staff yelling behind him that Kaimen was the one with the gun but he ignored them.

"Ario?"

A cop stepped up behind the officer who had his gun drawn on us.

"Officer Montoya, I'm glad to see you for a change."

"Put your gun down. These doctors aren't a threat. What happened here Ario?"

"My brother pulled a gun on all of us. Basically, held us hostage. We felt the situation escalating so me and my dad tried to wrestle the gun out of his hands. It went off. We weren't sure who was hit until just now."

"I can't stop the bleeding," my dad said smearing his glasses with blood.

A puddle formed under Kaimen. The only one in the room praying he wouldn't die was my father. The rest of us our emotions were like a blank canvas. We didn't feel either way about him living or dying.

It was a cold thing to think but I prayed he would die. Even if he went to prison, we would always wonder if he was going to try and kill us the first chance he got.

What they say about one bad apple spoiling the bunch was true. None of us were saints but Kaimen had deeper seated issues that ate away at our family. Prayerfully he can find the peace in death that he never found in life.

We all played a part in each other's destruction one way or another.

THE END